Molting

Kathryn Tennison

UNCOMFORTABLY DARK HORROR

Book Cover Design and wrap by Christy Aldridge of Grim Poppy Design

First edition 2025

Edited & formatted by 360 Editing, a division of Uncomfortably Dark Horror.

Editors: Candace Nola & Mort Stone

Published by Uncomfortably Dark Horror, owned and operated by Candace Nola. Pittsburgh, PA

Follow us on all social media, our Patreon, or on our website to stay up to date on new releases, appearances, and more!

Committed to *"bringing you the best in horror, one uncomfortably dark page at a time."*

Patreon www.patreon.com/c/u12231330

Website www.uncomfortablydark.com

CONTENTS

incredible storytelling!"—Somer Canon, author of YOU'RE MINE

"Gripping and Intense, filled with emotional depth and vivid imagery, this story will linger within you long after the book is closed."—Daemon Manx, author of The Ojanox series

"Molting is suspenseful, shock-inducing body horror dug right out of a secret room in the basement of an abandoned house, reminiscent of T. Kingfisher's "The Twisted Ones" only ten times as spine-chilling. Kathryn Tennison is a unique voice in horror who is now permanently on my Want-To-Read list!"—Jill Girardi, Owner, Kandisha Press

"What a wicked spin on the haunted house story! MOLTING portrays a descent into madness in authentic and terrifying ways other books can only dream of. Tennison has crafted a pitch-black rumination on what it means to lose yourself and never lets the reader find their footing for a second."—B rennan LaFaro, author of the SLATTERY FALLS trilogy

DEDICATION

For Salem – your adventurous, courageous spirit will never stop inspiring me.

PART ONE: MIGRATING

---

*"I felt glad as the road shortened before me: so glad
that I stopped once to ask myself what that joy
meant: and to remind reason that it was not to my
home I was going, or to a permanent resting-place,
or to a place where fond friends looked out for me
and waited my arrival."—Jane Eyre*

Chapter 1

In the darkness, I nearly slipped down the steep bank into the black water. These woods were unfamiliar, and I had been scanning the night sky as I walked, searching for the Cygnus constellation, when my well-worn sneakers hit a slick mat of damp leaves and pine needles.

It was more of a slide than a fall. My feet slithered over the edge of the drop-off to the river, and I gently sat back on the cold ground, all the way down, rocks and tree roots jutting into me, until I was flat on my back, staring straight up.

"I thought there would be more stars," I said. "And more noise."

Propping myself up on my elbows, I looked down at the rushing water. Whitecaps popped up here and there, little eddies, but they were oddly silent, even as they lapped against the large rocks protruding near the shoreline. There were no cricket chirps or bird songs. Even the occasional whoosh of passing cars from the road I'd traveled to get here did not intrude beyond the barrier of trees.

Heart still pounding, I pushed myself up into a sitting position and rested with my back against a tree and my legs dangling over the drop, taking deep breaths through my nose. What the forest lacked in sights and sounds, it made up for in smells – musky pine, wet earth, damp wood, smoke from a nearby fire.

Across the river was a small house, only the second I'd seen during my long walk.

Will I be okay out here?

An impossible question. What did "okay" even mean anymore? Happy? Healthy? Simply alive?

A rustling noise made me turn my head. Too loud to be a squirrel or a rabbit or even a fox, yet it didn't sound like human footsteps. An enormous, shaggy shape emerged from a cluster of scraggly bushes, something long and furry dangling from its mouth.

"Monster?"

A muffled *woof*, and my shoulders relaxed.

"Did you catch another squirrel?" I accused. "I told you to leave them alone."

Monster's fluffy tail drooped, and he dropped the squirrel, which landed on the ground with a soft, wet thump. Then he ambled up to me like a kid caught in the act of coloring on the walls. He lay down beside me, put his head between his paws, and stared at me with mournful brown eyes.

"You big dope," I said, scratching his floppy black ears affectionately. "I'm not mad. But if we're going to make this our home, you can't go around killing all the neighbors."

My phone showed that it was 8:40 PM, and that I had no service, which suited me fine. There was nobody I wanted to talk to aside from Chloe, and she was still driving her final stretch to California. But my dad would be calling soon (in fact, he probably had already), and he would worry if I didn't answer.

Once more, I searched for Cygnus. Once more, it eluded me.

"Come on, boy." I stood, dusting off the seat of my baggy jeans. "Let's head back."

We turned to go, and the lights in the house across the river flicked off, leaving the woods a little darker.

As I navigated the overgrown trail, Monster at my heels, the night seemed to come back to life. A white-tailed rabbit darted away; an ambulance siren wailed faintly; in the distance, headlights flashed. I was glad for that. Much as I wanted to be on my own for a while, I didn't love the idea of total isolation.

A few minutes later, I heard a snatch of laughter. When I crested a small hill, I realized I had reached my new neighbor's house – neighbor being a relative term, since our houses were still almost a mile apart. Fire blazed in the pit in his backyard. Pizza boxes and a red cooler sat on a rickety picnic table, ready for a party, yet nobody was around.

The laugh came again, louder and closer. I barely had time to step back into the trees before my neighbor, an elderly man named Lester, appeared around the side of the house, laughing uproariously. Monster let out a low growl at the sudden approach.

"Shh," I hissed.

Lester froze. "Hello?"

The silence stretched uncomfortably. Keeping a tight grip on Monster's leash, I debated revealing myself.

Too late. He's going to think I'm a total creep if I speak up now.

"Simon?" said Lester in a hushed voice, gazing up into the trees and turning in a slow circle. "Is that you? Have you come back for me?"

He made a compulsive movement with his hand, almost like the sign of the cross, and said: "Up, down, up, down. Left, right, left, right."

Then he beat his palm against the side of his head as though trying to get water out of his ear, took a slice of pizza from one of the boxes, and disappeared inside.

"Okay," I said slowly, glancing up at the branches and seeing nothing. "Note to self: watch out for that guy. And for Simon, whoever or whatever he is."

Clutching my coat tighter around me, I returned to the main path. This was a level of cold I'd never experienced in September. Indiana had had pretty low temperatures, but this New Hampshire chill pierced to the bone, gripping so tightly it was hard to shake it off.

I picked up the pace, eager to be home.

Home – I've never thought of it like that.

The word didn't fit yet. Could a house be called a home when it wasn't suitable to live in? When the paperwork had only been signed a few hours ago? When nobody was waiting there for you to return? Well, that last part wasn't quite true. My friend Spencer was there. But coming home to him and a heap of boxes wasn't like coming home to family.

A round stone well appeared suddenly out of the darkness, and I knew I was almost there. After the well came the little slope leading to the outdoor fireplace with its ash-blackened bricks, and then I could see the simple A-frame jutting like a bird's beak from the trees.

Just then, a dark shape flitted across my peripheral vision, and Monster let loose a single, booming bark that shook the very air. I watched the creature as it landed in a nearby pine, thinking it was an owl, but the shape wasn't quite right.

I was still staring at it when my phone vibrated and chimed half a dozen times. Now that I had service again, all the missed calls and texts bombarded me.

"Come on," I said to Monster, but he didn't budge.

He was focused on the shape in the tree, and he was making a noise I'd never heard before, halfway between a growl and a whimper.

"Monster," I commanded. "Inside. Now."

Reluctantly, he tore his gaze away from the mystery bird and followed me into our new home.

One of the reasons I had fallen in love with the A-frame house was the back wall made entirely of glass. The house itself was far from impressive – two stories, three small bedrooms, tiny kitchen – but that triangular window with its view of the river and mountains was priceless. Of course, right now, dust and grime coated the glass, and there was a spiderweb crack like a bird had crashed into it. Another item on the endless list of tasks necessary to make this place habitable.

The wooden steps up to the back deck groaned as I climbed them. Lights were on inside, but somehow they made the house gloomier, illuminating its many problems.

"I was ten minutes away from calling a search and rescue team," said Spencer when I walked through the door. "I thought maybe Lester had snatched you."

"He does have a snatcher-type name."

"Seriously. Why would anyone name their child Lester?"

"Maybe the name predestined him to a life of creepiness."

Spencer snorted. "He's really not that bad, though. He always says hi to me at the grocery store, though, come to think of it, I haven't seen him there in a while. Huh."

"And does he often laugh to himself and have solitary pizza parties like the one I just witnessed?"

"Who knows?" Spencer said with a wink. "Maybe he'll invite you next time."

"Lucky me."

Spencer fell silent and bent to scratch Monster's ears. He hadn't asked a lot of questions about why I had made the sudden move from Indiana to New Hampshire, or even why I'd chosen to purchase a sixty-year-old fixer-upper in the woods. I knew he must be curious. But I wasn't ready to talk about it quite yet.

"By the way," I said to break the tension. "Do you know a Simon?"

"Hmm. Not that I can think of."

"I thought everyone around here knew everyone else," I teased.

"Usually. But some people move here to disappear into the woods and not have to talk to anybody."

Was he being hypothetical, or was he talking about me?

"Well," I continued, "he must come out of the woods to visit Lester, because that's who Lester thought I was."

"Interesting. Lester the creep and Simon the feral forest-man."

"They'd make an awesome super-villain duo."

My phone buzzed again. I'd already forgotten about the messages.

"I should settle in for the night," I said. "My dad's also ten minutes away from calling a search and rescue team if I don't talk to him."

"You're not actually sleeping in here, are you?" asked Spencer, his eyes traveling up to the sizable hole near the peak of the ceiling.

"I thought I'd camp out, even though it's freezing." I shivered at the thought. "I've never had any desire to live in California, but right now I'm almost jealous of my sister. It's got to be eighty degrees there."

"I've always liked the cold," said Spencer with a shrug. "And if you think it's cold now, just wait."

"Yeah," I sighed, looking up at the hole in the ceiling and the crack in the glass wall. "I'm on a tight deadline if I'm going to insulate this place before winter hits."

"You know, you could always come back to my place and stay there until the house is fixed up. And before you protest, it's no trouble. I really like having you two there."

He ruffled Monster's ears again. It was a tempting offer. *Very* tempting, when I thought about how cold it had been on my walk. Reconnecting with Spencer had been the best part of moving here. We hadn't been in touch much since college, but we had immediately fallen back into our old friendship. Most of it.

"Thanks," I said. "Seriously. But I think I need a little time to myself to figure things out."

"Fair enough." He squeezed my shoulder. "Before I go, how about a toast?"

Spencer went into the kitchen, which didn't have any appliances or a working sink, stove, or oven, and returned carrying a bottle of whiskey with a bright red bow on the front. My stomach lurched, but I forced a smile.

"It's your favorite, right?" he asked, twisting off the cap and pouring a measure of mahogany liquid into two tumblers. "At least it used to be."

"It still is." I accepted a glass, encircling it with trembling fingers. "What are we toasting to?"

"To this godforsaken house, and to the woman crazy enough to think she can fix it."

The words were meant to be charming, and I returned his grin, but I didn't like being called crazy, even in jest.

"It's not too late to back out," Spencer added more seriously. "As you know from rejecting place after place over the last three weeks, there are lots of houses around here that aren't so...rustic."

"I like it."

"Hey, whatever floats your boat. If anyone can turn this place around, it's you."

I brought the glass to my lips and pretended to drink. Not a single drop passed through, though the proximity and the smell were enough to make sweat break out on the back of my neck. Discreetly, I wiped my mouth rather than licking my lips. Spencer, who had drained his entire glass, didn't seem to notice.

"I'll leave this with you," he said, holding out the bottle. "Homeowner."

"Take it," I insisted. "I'll be handling all kinds of power tools, so that's not a great combination."

It was a stupid excuse, but that was one nice thing about Spencer – he didn't pry. He said goodnight and left through the front door, which swung shut behind him with a bone-rattling slam. Monster jolted out of a doze and grumbled.

"Door damper," I said. "Add it to the list."

Chapter 2

My phone stared at me accusingly from the poorly laminated kitchen counter next to the tumbler of whiskey, which looked more delicious by the second. I would've poured it down the sink, but the pipes underneath were connected to nothing but thin air. How was it that the scent of the alcohol permeated my nose even from several feet away?

"It's just one glass! Besides, you're not an alcoholic unless you drink before noon."

That's what my ex-husband, Daniel, had said often. Then, when we'd started drinking before noon, he'd made excuses for that, too.

Opening the back door, I splashed the whiskey onto the deck. The wood was half-rotted anyway; a little Wild Turkey wouldn't hurt it. Part of me wished I could toss the phone out as well, but it was still there when I turned around, innocuous in its plain, forest green case.

The screen lit up with a stutter, revealing the name *Daddy-o*.

"Hey, Dad," I answered cheerfully, as if I hadn't spent the last hour ignoring his calls.

"Hey, Michelle," he said, as if he hadn't been about to call the cops and report me as missing. "You back at Spencer's?"

"Actually," I said slowly, "I bought a house."

"Oh, yeah? You told me yesterday that you weren't having any luck."

Muffled conversations on his end told me that he was filling my mom in.

"Yeah, well, I finally found one I like. It needs a little work, but that's what I wanted. The realtor showed it to me this morning, and I just fell in love with it."

"Did you really think it through?"

"I did," I said, my enthusiasm waning. "It wasn't an impulse buy. I'm happy with it."

There was a pause. "Then I'm happy for you, Misha. All moved in yet?"

"Pretty much," I said, glancing at the small pile of boxes, plastic tubs, and duffel bags in the corner.

In the background, my mom said, "Tell her to send pictures!"

"Your mom wants you to send pictures," Dad repeated dutifully.

"And tell her to text us the address."

"She also wants the address."

"Sure," I said, knowing that if my mom saw the state of this place, she'd show up with a fumigation mask, a demolition crew, and printouts of all the acceptable housing options in the area.

"Let me talk to her." There was a muffled thump, and then my mom was on the line. "Have you heard from Chloe?"

"I don't know. Cell reception isn't great out here. Just check her location on your phone."

"I did, and she's in Burbank."

"Okay, that's good then. That's where her new apartment is."

"Oh – wait a second. She just texted that she made it. I'm gonna go call her."

Another thump, and my dad was back. "She misses you girls," he said. "It's hard for her, not being able to just walk up the stairs and see you."

"We know why Chloe wants to go to LA, for the acting and all that, but why do you *have to go so far?"*

That was one of many questions my mom had asked before I set out three weeks ago. I hadn't had a good answer back then, and I didn't really have one now. Not one that I was willing to tell them. And it was hard for me, too, with them a thousand miles away and Chloe triple that.

"What are you up to?" I asked, shifting the phone to my other ear. "It's Friday night – did everyone come over for pizza?"

"They're still here. Actually, Ava wants to talk to you. Hold on."

"When are you coming home?" a voice demanded not two seconds later. Unlike my father, my niece Ava had no filter.

"I live in New Hampshire now, remember?" I said.

"My dad says there's nothing in New Hampshire except creaky old houses and cemeteries, and he says you'll give up and come back, and Aunt Chloe will too."

Thanks, bro.

If Chloe could hear this, I knew exactly what she'd say: *"Hey Ava, tell your dad he's a dick."* She was also of the no-filter persuasion. I, on the other hand, felt a little bad for Ava. Recently, she had reached the age where her younger siblings were pests and her parents were lame; but Chloe and I, the young, hip aunts, were the height of cool. And then we'd both left with barely any notice.

When I hung up the phone a few minutes later, the silence and emptiness of the house pressed against me, the darkness of the woods beyond like a vast ocean. If only I hadn't dumped out that whiskey. I checked my texts, hoping for a message from the only person who would sympathize – Chloe.

There was one text:

C: LA is so rad, or whatever word you old people use these days

It was accompanied by a selfie of Chloe smiling outside her new apartment building, her long, honey-blonde hair molten in the sunshine. A pang went through me. How could I already miss her so much? Wiping my eyes, I typed a response.

M: We actually prefer "groovy".

<hr>

"Camping? Stupid idea," I said the instant I stepped outside to set up my tent.

I thought I'd been prepared for the change in climate, but there weren't enough coats and wool socks in the world to insulate me against this wicked New England chill. Yet somehow, my phone said it was only 62 degrees.

"Liar," I said, shoving it into my pocket.

Maybe I needed time to adapt, and maybe it would be okay to sleep inside, and so what if the roof fell in on me? At least I wouldn't die a Popsicle. And if I died, I wouldn't have to deal with what the doctor had told me a month ago.

"You may experience difficulty making decisions," she'd said. *"Even simple ones like what to eat for dinner."*

Or where to sleep.

"Camping it is," I said to Monster, whose impenetrable fluff would've kept him warm in Antarctica.

Chloe and I had camped a lot this past summer, and I was well-practiced at putting the tent together. It was fairly cozy once I tossed in blankets and pillows and built a fire in the outdoor fireplace. Still, I couldn't help imagining Chloe lounging on the beach in shorts and a crop top with a warm breeze on her face.

"Lucky West Coast bitch," I muttered affectionately, pulling on another layer of socks.

The stars were still not as numerous or as bright as I'd expected, but I continued the search for Cygnus nonetheless. Before Chloe and I parted ways three weeks ago, she said:

"We should pick a constellation, and then we can both look up at it and think about each other, and even though we'll be on opposite coasts, we'll be able to see the same stars at the same moment."

She'd said it with such earnestness that I quickly agreed, choosing not to burst her bubble by pointing out that by the time she could see the stars in LA, I would be asleep. On our final camping trip, in early August, we borrowed a friend's telescope and looked for a constellation that was easy to spot, settling on Cygnus, the swan. Then Chloe begged me to get matching swan tattoos or constellation tattoos or star tattoos. We never found a design that looked exactly right.

Now, squinting up at the sky, searching for Cygnus, I wished we'd gotten tattoos after all. Skin and ink were more reliable than far-off celestial orbs, too distant to touch.

Monster's soft, warm presence had helped me through a lot of restless nights and hung-over mornings, but being in this unfamiliar place with its unfamiliar sounds and smells made sleep difficult. I kept jolting upright, convinced that there was someone standing right outside my tent. Logically, I knew that a stranger couldn't get within ten yards of me without Monster noticing, and yet...

The first thing I realized upon waking was that my socks were gone.

My feet must've gotten hot while I slept, but now they were freezing and rigid. Without opening my eyes, I wiggled my stiff toes. As I sat up, my bones creaked and my neck cracked, and it hit me that I was no longer in the tent. I couldn't even *see* the tent. Surrounded by trees, I was lying in between the protruding roots of a large elm with no memory of how I had gotten there.

The back of my neck itched, and my hand itched, and—

Oh my god, I'm covered in ants!

Jumping up, I swatted the little menaces off every inch of exposed skin (thankfully, there were few), and why weren't those fuckers in hibernation? Or better yet, frozen dead? When I reached down to sweep another one off my bare foot, I saw the dark stain between the roots of the tree, and I smelled blood. Apparently, the ants had awakened for a midnight feast. But what had left the blood?

"Monster?" I called, my voice tiny in the still night.

There was no reply, and I couldn't see him anywhere.

"Monster!"

It took a moment for me to orient myself. That dreadful feeling of not knowing where I was sent twisting cramps through my stomach as I lurched awkwardly away from the entangling roots, nearly falling several times, my numb feet about as useful as stumps.

At last, I heard the river, and I walked with it on my right until I reached my little campsite. My socks (all three pairs) were lying half in and half out of the open tent flap. I snatched them up and tugged them back on, massaging my frigid feet. Other than the socks, pillows, and blankets, the tent was empty.

My doom-inclined heart pumped horrific ideas into my brain: Monster slipping into the river and drowning; Monster chasing a squirrel into the road and getting hit by a truck; Monster only existing inside my head.

You saw Spencer pet him, I reminded myself. *He's real. Don't get fucking crazy right now. You're not that far gone.*

My phone, ten percent away from death, was my only light as I circled the house, shouting Monster's name. The freestanding garage was locked up tight, and the stone cover remained securely on the well. Had it always been that far to the right, though? Yes. Probably. I was about to search the boxes for my actual flashlight when the same bird I had seen earlier soared out of the woods and landed on the deck railing. Or was it a bat?

Momentarily distracted, I stepped closer. The winged creature immediately took off, coming to rest on the outdoor brick fireplace. When I moved forward, it did the same thing again, landing in a tree at the edge of the drop-off to the river.

"Do you...want me to follow you?" I asked, feeling ridiculous as soon as the words left my lips.

The creature made no sound. As I stared up at it, a single dark feather fell, brushing my cheek before dropping to my shoulder.

"A bird after all."

I picked it up gingerly and was about to hold it in the beam of light when my phone died. At the same moment, a rustling of wings told me that the bird had left once more. Only then did I snap out of it and remember what I was supposed to be doing.

Faint growling was coming from the north side of the property, which I hadn't seen much of, and which the realtor had eagerly informed me contained a hiking trail. Doing my best not to fall, I followed the sound, nearly crying with relief when Monster's bulky form came into view. He was crouched low, focused on a hole at the base of a lichen-spotted boulder.

"You little shit," I said, nudging him gently with my leg. "What are you doing over here?"

Finally, he looked at me. Then he whined and looked back at the ground, pawing at it.

"It's a hole, buddy. They happen sometimes."

When I tried to pull him away, he resisted, straining at his collar.

"I did not pay hundreds of dollars on obedience school for this rebellion," I said sternly. "We're going home. Now."

His reluctant gaze seemed to say, *"But where is home? Where is my soft bed and my pig-shaped chew toy?"* Grabbing his collar, I dragged him away from the lair of whatever poor animal he'd been tormenting, brought him back to the tent, and zipped us both inside.

I remembered everything now. Of course I did. It had gotten stuffy inside the tent, so I had unzipped it and taken my socks off. Then I had to pee, so I went into the woods and found that tree, but I'd been distracted looking for Cygnus again and must've fallen asleep. I hadn't slept well in days, so it wasn't surprising.

Monster curled up beside me, but I could tell he was still on alert. Before I fell asleep, I took the feather out of my pocket and twirled it between my fingers, thinking about how it had been dead long before the bird let it go.

CHAPTER 3

EVEN THOUGH I'D SLEPT poorly, I inevitably woke at six the next morning. The fact that I wasn't even groaning about it told me just how old I was getting. Six AM on a weekend, and I was eager to get up and start the day. Chloe would've been disgusted.

Monster sat patiently by the closed tent flap, waiting to be released. As soon as I unzipped it, he darted outside, looking for a place to do his business. Out of habit, I folded the blankets, set them on the pillows, and placed the whole stack neatly in a corner. When I stepped out into the brisk air, I zipped the tent behind me, wondering how long I'd have to use it.

Amazing how just a few months ago, I'd been living in a four-bedroom, three-bathroom house with my (now ex) husband Daniel, and now I was sleeping in a tent with my dog and peeing in the woods. It would've been funny if it hadn't made my insides writhe.

After rebuilding the fire, I hunted through boxes to find my blue-and-white tin coffee pot. While I was searching, I came across my flashlight and held it for a minute, frowning. Didn't I need this for something? I couldn't remember, so I set it aside and kept digging. No matter how ruggedly I was living at the moment, coffee was still a priority. I wasn't a savage. Although I did have to drink it black.

With my steaming mug in hand, I went to the truck and let it run for a while in order to charge my phone. The seats of the truck weren't yet molded to my shape, and sometimes it still felt like I was driving a rental. Daniel always made fun of people who drove trucks, so it had given me a bit of savage pleasure when I bought it, knowing I would need it for the move. It had given me even more savage pleasure to see Daniel's tight-lipped expression when he saw it the day I went back to the house to pack up the rest of my belongings.

My phone buzzed when it came to life, and I saw a text from Chloe from last night—a blurry picture of the night sky with the caption, *CYGNUS!!!* I zoomed in as far as I could, but the stars were nothing more than washed-out smudges. I'd have to take her word for it.

She was thinking about me, just like I was thinking about her.

Often, she wouldn't text me for days at a time, and I would stupidly start to worry that she'd forgotten me. Maybe now that we were both in new places where we hardly knew anybody, we'd rely on each other more. She wasn't a recluse like me, though. She was ten years younger and much better at making friends. Before long, she might not need me anymore.

Remembering the time difference, I spent ten minutes searching for the perfect swan GIF but didn't send it yet. Then, I opened my email. The connection was spotty, and it took a while for the five new emails to load. While I waited, I reached into my pocket for the feather from last night, but it was gone.

Two of the emails were spam, one was a newsletter from a dog rescue charity I'd donated to a few times, one was regarding some final paperwork for the house, and the last was from my favorite co-worker from my previous job as an architect.

Hey Michelle,

How is New Hampshire? I hope it sucks, because things here have been terrible since you left. Last week, I printed three – 3!

– personal pages and you-know-who lost it. Seriously, it cost less than a dollar total. So, if you need any help visualizing your plans for that fixer-upper you've been searching for, let me know. I'd be more than happy to use the expensive company design software for you.

Also...just a heads up...Daniel called here the other day asking if we had a forwarding address for you because he had something to send. Said he thought you might've given it to us so we could mail your last paycheck, as if he doesn't know that's all done electronically. Honestly, it was strange. Maybe you should reach out to him? Unless he cheated on you. Then fuck him. Not prying, promise.

Anyway, let me know when you find a place. And let me know about the software.

Sooner rather than later, because I'm not sure how much longer I can do this job without you.

XO, Lauren

I read the paragraph about Daniel four times, and it still didn't make sense. Why would he contact my old office to ask about my address? For that matter, why was he asking about my address at all? We had finalized our divorce in July, over two months ago, and it had been an amicable split. What could he possibly have to send me?

The more I stared at the email, the weirder it was. After a while, even Daniel's name became an unrecognizable blob of letters.

RAPID, BOOMING BARKS. I glanced up from my phone in time to see Monster barreling towards a pale, spindly figure in coveralls – Lester.

"Monster, stop!" I shouted, leaping from the truck. "Down!"

By the time I reached them, Lester was half crouched with his arms wrapped over his mostly bald head.

"I'm so sorry," I said, getting a firm hold on Monster's collar. "He's very protective. Can I help you?"

"I only come over to see how you're — how you're settling in," Lester said, still in his defensive position. "This house has been empty a long time, and it always looked forlorn-like."

"It's still pretty forlorn."

"Got more life in it now, though. Seen smoke from your fire and smelled the coffee."

Something in me softened. He may have been odd, especially given what I'd witnessed the night before, but he was old and probably lonely and seemed to have good intentions. When I left Indiana, I told myself I needed to leave Indiana Michelle behind as well. She'd always been too accommodating. She would've gone out of her way to be neighborly to Lester, even if she didn't want to. But maybe there was a halfway point between Indiana Michelle and Total Bitch Michelle.

"Maybe we could grab a cup sometime," I said, smiling. "You could tell me about the neighborhood."

"Ain't so much a neighborhood. But I'd appreciate the cup all the same."

"Another time," I said. "I should get going. Obviously, I still have a lot of work to do on the house. I've got to order materials, re-key the locks—"

"No need for locks around here," Lester said as he finally straightened up. I noticed that his back was slightly hunched. "Safest area in the country."

"You don't lock your doors?"

"Nobody does."

I found that hard to believe. Occasionally, Daniel had left doors unlocked, not on purpose but carelessly. A little thrill of terror had shot through me every time I came home to find that the house wasn't secure and hadn't been all day. It was like missing a step on a staircase, expecting one thing but discovering another, darker truth.

"Got all the tools you need to fix this place up?" Lester asked, nodding at the house.

"I think so," I lied. "And I can get anything else from a hardware store."

"I got an old table saw in my garage. Nothing pretty, but it gets the job done."

"Oh, that's okay," I said quickly. "I'd like to have one of my own anyway."

"Well, how about I give it to you? I ain't used it in ten years."

"No, I couldn't possibly accept it."

"Consider it a housewarming gift."

He smiled, revealing a missing tooth. The wrinkled skin around his brown eyes crinkled even more, in a very well-worn, earnest kind of way, and maybe he wasn't such a creep after all.

"Okay," I said. "If you're sure."

"You go on and do whatever you need to do, and I'll bring it by tomorrow, leave it on the porch."

"Thank you."

As I watched him leave (he was surprisingly spry for a man who had to be at least 75), I wondered if he had any friends or family nearby to check on him. I was fairly certain he lived alone. Would that be me in forty years? Still all alone out here in the woods, craving even a scrap of human interaction? Or would I grow to like solitude so much that I wouldn't even miss people?

———◆———

I COULDN'T EXPLAIN, EVEN to myself, why I liked this run-down triangle of a house. The local realtor Spencer recommended had taken me to dozens of other houses, and some of them had even been fixer-uppers like I wanted, but none of them had felt right.

"Well, I only have one more house listed at the moment," she had said hesitantly. "But it hasn't been occupied in years, decades really, and I'm afraid it's a real mess."

The moment I saw it, I fell in love. It was a wreck, sure, but there was a certain charm about the pointy A-frame poking up toward the sky, trees and mountains reflected in its glass wall. It was almost like I had seen the house in a long-ago dream, only remembering the dream when I saw the house in real life. There was something familiar about it. Through all the disrepair and disuse, I saw myself living there – morning coffee on the deck, long hikes with Monster, cooling my feet in the river in summer.

"I'm an architect," I had told Spencer. "If there's anything I know how to fix, it's houses."

"Isn't it the contractors that do the actual work, though?" he'd said.

He was right, of course. Yet I hoped and trusted that my architectural skills (and some research) would be all that I needed.

Once Lester was gone, I went to get my flashlight, notebook, and pencil so I could start my official inspection and list of repairs.

"Priority number one," I said, hitting the flashlight with my palm so it would stop flickering. "Electricity."

I wrote it at the top of the list and continued inside. A light drizzle had started. Monster settled in the corner of the main room, looking slightly anxious. He didn't like storms. Come to think of it, neither did I, especially when a slight breeze might knock the whole house down.

"It'll be fine," I said, not sure if I was speaking to Monster or to myself. "We're safe."

Next on the list were water, gas, and internet, though truthfully, I didn't care too much about that last one. Part of my reason for moving here had been to reconnect with nature. Far too much of my life had been spent scrolling through my phone and staring at a computer screen at work. Rather than keep people guessing by removing all my photos of Daniel, I had simply deleted my social media accounts. So far, I hadn't missed them one bit.

I scratched out "internet" on the list, then tore the whole page out of the notebook and crumpled it up. Going room by room would be easier and more organized.

The back part of the house, the part facing the river, was one big, open area – a living room, a dining nook, a kitchen separated from the rest only by the mid-height counters, and a loft above. At least, I assumed there was a loft up there. The spiral staircase had long ago collapsed into a pile of rust, so I had never actually seen it.

Knees groaning, I sat down beside Monster and wrote a new list:

General items:
Electricity
Re-key locks
Gas
Water
Fix hole in roof
New roof shingles
Internet (?)

Living room:
Crack in glass wall
Replace spiral staircase
New floors

Kitchen:
Pipes under sink
Connections for stove and oven
Replace countertops
Sand/paint cabinets
New appliances

Loft: ????

<u>Downstairs bedroom</u>:

"Shit. Shit, shit, fuck."

Overwhelmed, I stood and paced around the living room, each creak of the floorboards threatening to send me over the edge. It was too much. Way too much. How had I ever believed I could handle this alone? Or at all? Just because I had redone one of the bathrooms at mine and Daniel's house did not mean I was qualified for this.

Sensing my distress, Monster whined softly.

"I'm sorry," I said, sitting down again and stroking his side. "I'm sorry I got us into this mess."

Even though it was still on the early side in LA, I got out my phone and sent the GIF I'd found earlier to Chloe, silently begging her to respond right away. My foot started tapping, and I couldn't seem to make it stop. To my relief, Chloe's text came only a few minutes later.

C: Ha! Love it
M: You're up early (and by early I mean at a normal hour).
C: Guess I'm not used to the time change yet
M: I still woke up at 6 this morning...
C: Ugh. OLD.
M: Rude.
M: What are your plans for today?
C: Iced coffee, job-hunting with Fabi probably.
M: Fabi?
C: Fabiola. One of my new roomies. What about you?
M: Hardware store.
C: I repeat – OLD
M: The house I bought isn't in great shape, gonna have to fix it up.
C: You bought a house?? Since when?!
M: Yesterday.
C: Pics???

M: Not until it's a little less...shitty.

We continued to text for a while, and I debated whether to tell her just how awful the house was and how panic was paralyzing me. But what could she do to help? She was three thousand miles away, spending time with people I'd never heard of and would probably never meet.

Come on, don't get jealous. You're her sister. You're irre-placeable.

Whether that was true or not, my conversation with Chloe helped settle my anxious mind. I added a few more items to the list and then continued down the hall that opened up between the kitchen and dining area. This hall had a small bedroom on the right, and a utility closet and bathroom on the left. The bedroom wasn't terrible (except for the ancient floral comforter), but the bathroom would need a lot of work, and the utility closet wouldn't open no matter how hard I pushed it.

To the left of the front door with its glass storm door (remembering last night, I wrote "door damper" on the list) was a staircase. I had been up it once before when I viewed the house, and it hadn't exactly been stable. It also hadn't collapsed, though, so I decided to risk it.

Each step groaned as if my weight caused it immense pain. When I tried to grab onto the railing, it came loose from the wall, metal brackets cracking, and the whole staircase shook when it fell.

"Shit!"

Frozen, I waited for the stairs to crumble out from under me. They didn't, so I continued.

On the second floor was a narrow landing, an even narrow-er hall, and two more bedrooms, one on each side. Walking to the end of the pitch-black hall, I knocked on the wall. The loft was on the other side, and going through this wall might be the best way to reach it.

There was a creak behind me, and I turned, ready to scold Monster for following me, but he wasn't there.

The bedroom on the left had a metal-framed, mattress-less bed in one corner and a shattered light fixture in the other. No window. Three locks had been fastened to the outside of the other bedroom door – a chain lock, a sliding door latch, and a padlock hasp (minus the padlock). They looked like the newest parts of the house, still shiny and sturdy. None of them were locked, yet when I tried to open the door, it wouldn't budge. I rammed my shoulder against it like I'd seen in movies, resulting only in a burst of pain. Then I tried a kick, and then a second kick, which did the trick.

This bedroom was even smaller than the others, more like a walk-in closet, but it did have a window with long, maroon curtains. My heart stopped. One of the curtains bulged in an unmistakable way – somebody was hiding behind it.

Without thinking, I threw my hefty flashlight at the curtain. It thunked against the wall and crashed to the floor, hitting something that made a hollow, metallic sound. Ripping the curtain back, I saw a small trash can.

Exhaling a laugh, I picked up the flashlight and closed the curtains.

"Okay, crazy lady. If you're going to live on your own, you can't be so jumpy."

Notes complete, I turned to head back downstairs, and that's when I saw the scratches carved into the inside of the bedroom door at a height of about eight inches. Kneeling, I brought the flashlight closer. When I lined my fingers up with the scratches, I realized that they couldn't have come from a human. They were too thin, too deep. More like claw marks.

Probably just a pet cat or a dog. Not unusual.

But then I took a second look at the multitude of locks. Leaning closer to inspect them, I saw a smear of old blood on the padlock hasp.

What the hell were they keeping in here?

CHAPTER 4

BY THE TIME I was done making lists, it was too late in the day to venture into town. The rain had picked up, so I abandoned the idea of camping, packed the tent, and brought my things inside. Water dripped through the hole in the roof. Since I didn't have a bucket, I went carefully back upstairs, grabbed the trashcan that had frightened me so much, and positioned it to catch the drops.

"I know, boy," I said to Monster, who was staring out the glass wall. "It's miserable and cold. I swear I'll buy you a new bed tomorrow."

His tail gave a half-hearted wag, and I added "bed" and "treats" to my ever-expanding shopping list.

All I wanted was a hot meal, a soft seat, and an old movie like the ones Chloe loved. Instead, I had a peanut butter and jelly sandwich, a few defeated pillows, and the steady, unrelenting plunk of rain against metal.

That night, I dreamed about the house. I was walking down a nondescript road and happened to look over and see the A-frame poking above the trees. For some reason, I was convinced that the house was about to collapse, and that I could stop it by going inside and bracing the walls with my body. The inside of the house, however, was my house in Indiana. Not the one I'd shared with Daniel for nearly eight years, but the one I'd grown up in, the one my parents still lived in.

The layout was different, and I kept getting lost. Random pieces of furniture shouldn't have been there. Some rooms were too crowded for me to enter, and others were completely empty. Then a voice called out: "I'm in the cellar!" We didn't have a cellar, but I went outside and down some steps, and there it was. I tried to open the door, but it was held shut by a column of twenty different locks. The harder I tugged, the more locks appeared.

When the doorbell rang, I woke with a start, not sure if the noise had been in my dream or in real life.

The rain had stopped, and the house was eerily quiet. Thick white mist hid the trees. I waited, holding my breath, reminding myself that the doorbell wasn't even functional. My too-bright phone clock declared that it was 3:37 AM, and my rumbling stomach declared that it was still hungry. A box of seedy crackers was the only food I had. They left my mouth and throat dry, triggering a fit of coughing so violent that Monster raised his head in concern. I fumbled for my water bottle and knocked it over, sending it rolling across the floor.

At the back of my throat, something was triggering my gag reflex. Thinking it was a hair, I shoved my fingers past my teeth, nearly vomiting, and pulled out a feather, its bristles clumped with saliva, the tip of the shaft bloody.

On hands and knees, I crossed the room, snatched up my water bottle, and slid open the back door. I gargled and spat three times, then leaned against the wall to catch my breath. Monster came and stood beside me, and I buried my face in his musty fur.

"That was disgusting," I said hoarsely.

In the light of my phone, I examined the sticky feather. It was striped black and taupe, with one white splotch near the tip, just like the one that had fallen from the mystery bird. Was I at risk now of contracting terrible diseases? Bird flu? Blood in your mouth was never good, right?

Unfortunately, the closest hospital was a forty-five minute drive away. Also, even though I wasn't hurting for money, I needed every penny for the house. Without insurance, who knew how much a visit to the emergency room would cost?

Deciding that I was overreacting, I settled back on my makeshift bed with Monster next to me, his warmth comforting. The coppery taste of blood was still on my tongue, and my throat ached and itched. As I finally drifted off to sleep again, I thought I heard a faint scratching noise from upstairs.

EVERY TRACE OF MIST was gone when morning came. Sunlight streamed across the clear sky, and the air was fresh and cold. Since I planned on going into town as soon as possible, I didn't bother making a fire to heat up coffee. I desperately hoped there would be a cafe in Arden Woods, though I knew the town was tiny. According to Spencer, Arden Woods was "good for skiing, but not much else" and "full of the Northern brand of rednecks". Even rednecks drank coffee though, right?

While Monster ran loose in the yard, releasing his pent-up energy, I dug through boxes for something suitable to wear. Most of my business casual clothes had gone straight to charity after I quit my job. I had never felt comfortable in them, anyway. There was no need to dress up to go into town, but I at least wanted to not look like a person who had been sleeping in tents and on floors for two days.

At the very top of a box was an old pair of paint-spattered jeans given to me by Chloe.

"They're good luck," she had said, folding them sloppily and tossing them in the box as we both packed for our new lives.

"Didn't you wear them when you were working on the set for Sweeney Todd in high school?"

"Exactly. My blood, sweat, and tears went into those pants. And some fake blood, too."

"That's incredibly gross."

I had taken them anyway, and as I slid them on now, it was like Chloe was with me. She had always been the artistic one, the lead set painter and costume designer for all her high school plays. Many years before that, I had also been involved in my school plays, but I was the one building sliding floors and stairs that led to nowhere.

Both sets of skills – creative and practical – would be needed for this house. Maybe wearing Chloe's jeans would help me to think like her.

Because the pants were so colorful, I opted for a plain white shirt and a gray hooded sweatshirt coat that reached my knees. My hair, which was getting a little too long for my preference, got tamed into a braid and topped with a blue beanie my mother got me last Christmas.

"Monster! Here, boy!" I called as I laced up my boots, which I'd finally extracted from a box.

He followed me to the truck and hopped obediently into the passenger seat. While the butt warmers heated up, I plugged my phone in and searched for the hardware store Spencer had told me about. It wasn't hard to find, since it was the only one in a 30-mile radius.

"Hayden & Sons Hardware," I said, clicking on it. "Twenty-one minutes away. Not too bad."

Holes riddled the long gravel drive, making my truck and my bones rattle and bounce. I made a mental note to resurface it or maybe even pave it. At the end of the driveway was what Spencer had called the "main road", though in reality it was never very busy. The asphalt gleamed from last night's rain.

As I turned carefully onto the road, I messed with the radio dials, finally settling on a station playing old bluegrass, which seemed appropriate. I grinned to think of the way Chloe's lip would curl if she could hear the twangy banjo.

For a few miles, the road was empty, with nothing but woods on either side to attract my gaze. Then the speed limit dropped, and we passed through a small residential area with signs for a school bus stop. Beyond that, as the road climbed up into the mountains, yellow signs warned of falling rocks, and the temperature dropped five degrees.

I wouldn't want to come this way in the dead of winter.

When the road dipped again, I caught my first glimpse of the town of Arden Woods below. It was actually a little bigger than I'd expected. Multiple roads branched out from a white-steepled church. On the outskirts, small squares of farmland spread out like a patchwork quilt.

The temperature rose again as we headed down into the valley. A narrow, covered bridge spanned a river that glittered in the morning sun. On the other side was a large sign reading:

Welcome to Arden Woods!

Everyone is Home Here

<hr>

IF I HAD TRIED to imagine an adorable, family-owned hardware store in a perfectly quaint New England town, Hayden & Sons was exactly what I would've pictured.

The wooden exterior was pastel yellow, and the big front windows were decorated with hand-painted pumpkins and fall leaves. The Hayden & Sons sign over the door proudly declared that they had been *"Serving Arden Woods Since 1950"*. The parking lot was clean and well-paved, with just enough cars to tell me that the place did a good amount of business.

I cracked all the windows and left Monster in the front seat.

"Be good," I said, locking the car. "Don't throw any wild parties."

When I pushed open the front door, a cheery bell tinkled overhead. Several people milled around under fluorescent lights that somehow managed to be cozy rather than harsh. A woman in leggings and a baggy sweater stood near a display of autumn decor, a baby on one hip and a curly-haired toddler holding her free hand. The toddler smiled at me, and I smiled back before moving deeper into the store, consulting my list.

After several minutes of wandering, I ended up at a display of different types of nails. An employee was stocking shelves nearby, and I must've stared at the nails a little too long, because after a while she said:

"You look a little lost."

She was about my age with wild, curly black hair, a prominent nose, and rich brown eyes. Her orange vest had "H&S" embroidered on one side; under it, she wore a crisp white button-down.

"Uh, yeah," I said. "First time here."

"First time in Arden Woods, too, I'm guessing."

"How could you tell?" I asked, glancing around at the other shoppers to see if I really stood out from them that much.

"I know almost everybody around here. One of the perks of living in the same small town for your entire life."

That last sentence held only a trace of bitterness.

"Anyway," she said. "Welcome to Arden Woods, I guess. I'm Hannah Hayden."

"Hayden, as in Hayden and...sons?"

"Yeah, I guess 'Hayden & Sons & Daughter' didn't have as nice of a ring to it."

We both laughed. After two days of near-total isolation, it felt good to talk to someone, even if she was just helping me find the right kind of nails.

"So," Hannah said. "What all are you looking for? It must be a big project for you to get a cart."

"I'm afraid the cart won't even be big enough. I'm renovating a house."

"Really?" Hannah said with interest. "By yourself?"

"Yeah, I just bought this old A-frame on the river, and it needs serious help."

"What's the address? I'm not being creepy, I swear; I'm just curious which house it is."

"Oh, um..." I trailed off as the address flew out of my brain, despite the fact that I'd seen it a hundred times on the papers I signed. Helplessly, I gestured out the window toward the mountain I'd come down. "It's up that way. Sorry, I don't have the address memorized yet."

"Up the mountain? It can be dangerous out there in the winter. You should be careful."

The hairs on the back of my neck stood up. What did she mean by that?

"If you have an accident, it might take emergency services a bit to get to you," Hannah continued. "And cell service is unreliable up there."

"I'll be fine. I've got Monster to look out for me."

"Monster?"

"My dog."

Her eyes lit up. "What kind is he? Or she?"

"He's a Bernese mountain dog."

"Big dogs are the best."

"Especially when you're living alone."

The words hung awkwardly in the air. Clearing my throat, I returned to my list. Hannah guided me around the store, making recommendations on specific brands, telling me where to buy roof shingles, and suggesting a local electrician. I felt a strange reluctance to leave, even after I'd paid for my supplies. The idea of going back to my remote little house made my insides ache with loneliness.

"Do you have any kind of membership card?" I asked. "I'll be coming here a lot."

"Absolutely." She handed me a form and a pen, then said teasingly, "You can leave the address blank for now."

Once I had filled it out, she gave me a shiny orange plastic card with the Hayden & Sons logo on it. I tucked it into my wallet behind my driver's license, which reminded me that I would need a new license, and for that I would need to know my address. I *did* know it, though. Or at least, I thought I did.

"Is there anything else I can do for you?" Hannah asked, blowing a curl out of her face.

"Well, I've been living off sandwiches and crackers," I said. "Do you have any recommendations for a hot lunch?"

"There's a diner down the road. Don't eat the burgers, but their all-day breakfast is amazing. A little farther away is this new farm-to-table restaurant. I haven't eaten there yet, but I've heard good things. Or if you want to be more adventurous, there's a Thai place about three blocks that way."

She pointed.

"Great, thanks. Um, I guess I'll see you soon, probably."

"Good luck with the renovations!"

Even though there were more customers around, I felt Hannah's eyes on me all the way out of the store. Was it because she thought I was weird? Or because she was curious? Or had I actually, for the first time in almost a decade, managed to make a new friend?

Chapter 5

With the supplies loaded into the bed of my truck and a blue tarp tied securely over them, I climbed inside and cranked up the heat. Though it was nearly noon now, the day had barely warmed up.

Monster was wiggling in his seat, so I gave him some attention and let him lick my face. I could tell he was tired of being cooped up and eager to go home and chase squirrels, but I wasn't quite ready to go back yet. Going back meant I would have to get started on my work, and once I started my work, I would finally, irrevocably discover if I was capable of doing it.

Pulling onto what seemed to be the main road – Mill Street – I drove at a leisurely pace, taking in all the sights of my new town.

On the right were what looked to be multiple ski resorts, though their parking lots were almost empty. Skiing season didn't start until late November, apparently. On the left were old houses refurbished to be offices, restaurants, and stores. I took note of an insurance broker, a tax accountant, and a dentist. A bright pink house with peeling paint contained a New Age shop called Mystic Crystals. Clusters of quartz glinted on the stone steps and white windowsills.

At the sight of a corner cafe called Beans & Brews, I let out a sigh of relief, hurried inside, and ordered the biggest, darkest mocha possible. I also got a couple of plain scones and a small cup of whipped cream for Monster, who lapped it up so voraciously that little flecks peppered my jeans.

"People always say your name is a misnomer, but if they could see the way you devour whipped cream..."

A little farther down the road was the Thai restaurant, with warmly lit windows and a menu posted on the front door. The idea of hot, spicy noodles made my stomach growl. I ordered them to-go, hoping to get home before they were stone cold. But when I passed by a small grocery store, I decided to stop and pick up a few things.

Everything was fine until I reached the bread aisle. There was a specific brand I wanted, the brand I always got, but I suddenly couldn't remember the name. Starting on the top left, I scanned the rows and rows of loaves, looking for a color or logo that was familiar. I would get halfway through a row before realizing I hadn't finished the row above.

"Is there something I can help you find?" asked a middle-aged employee, giving me the kind of smile you wear for a child or confused grandparent.

"I'm, I just..." The words wouldn't come. My throat closed up around them.

"Are you okay?" the man asked, his smile fading slightly.

Get out of the bread aisle. Just pick something.

Grabbing a loaf at random, I dropped it in my cart, then wheeled the cart two aisles over, hoping the employee wouldn't follow. Covering my mouth with both hands, I coughed as quietly as I could. My throat hurt almost as badly as it had the night before, when I pulled out the feather.

There were bottles on the shelves, and I reached for one, thinking it was water, only to find myself holding 32 ounces of vodka. Hastily, I put it back. It was so cold in there. Why did they have the air conditioning on when it was freezing outside? My skin was dry and itchy.

Just go home.

Taking a deep breath that stung the back of my throat, I pushed my cart toward the end of the aisle, glancing one last time at the vodka.

THERE WAS BARELY ENOUGH room for the groceries in the backseat of the truck, but I managed to squeeze everything in. The sun had gotten much lower in the sky while I was in the store, and I wondered just how much time I'd spent staring at bread.

"Sunbeam," I said to Monster as we pulled out of the parking lot. "That's the brand. Fucking Sunbeam."

I rolled down the passenger window so he could stick his head out as we drove up into the mountains. He didn't seem to mind the cold at all, while I clutched my coat even tighter and turned the seat warmers up to maximum. Well, at least one of us was suited to the frigid mountain climate. Monster probably felt like he'd been waiting his whole life for this, like he was born for it. In fact, he *was* born for it.

If only it could've been that easy for me. If only I could've been sure I belonged here too.

Back up the mountain, back through the tiny suburbs. At the last second, I slammed on the brakes and turned into my driveway, nearly losing control of the truck as it bumped over the gravel.

"It's okay, buddy," I told both Monster and myself when we finally skidded to a stop. "We're okay."

Note to self: put some kind of sign or painted rock by the end of the driveway to make it more visible.

As soon as I opened the door, Monster jumped down from the truck and padded along the side of the house toward the backyard. I, meanwhile, had spotted something on the front porch. Only when I realized it was a table saw did I remember Lester's promise to bring it by. Honestly, I was ninety percent sure he would forget.

It was a high-quality, heavy-duty saw, and the blades were still sharp. From all the research I'd done on table saws, I estimated it was worth at least two thousand dollars, and it looked barely used, maybe even new.

A strange thought crossed my mind – had Lester bought this for me? No, that was insane. Why would he drop that much money on a total stranger? I wasn't sure whether the idea was creepy or sad. Wouldn't he rather spend money on people he loved? Or at least on himself?

The sudden urge to call Chloe flooded through me, and she must've been on the same wavelength, because at that moment my phone rang.

"Hey," I answered, wedging the phone between ear and shoulder and getting a few grocery bags out of the truck. "I was literally just thinking about you."

There was a pause so long I thought maybe it was a pocket-dial.

"Chlo?"

"So, um..."

From those two words alone, I could tell something was wrong. Her voice was thick and husky. I set the bags down on the gravel.

"What's going on?" I asked, leaning against the truck.

"Um, I hate it here."

"What?"

"I can't do this."

"LA is all you've talked about for years."

"Yeah, but actually being here? It's..." She sniffed. "It's not what I thought."

"Well, you've only been there two days. I'm sure it'll get better."

"No, it won't."

When Chloe got like this, there was no point in attempting to cheer her up. Everything I said, she would turn into a negative. Every encouragement would be shot down. It was frustrating at times. All I wanted was to fix it, and all she wanted was to wallow.

"Okay," I said soothingly. "Tell me what's wrong."

"The traffic sucks. I've almost gotten hit like five times already, and it takes me an hour to get anywhere. Everything is so fucking expensive. Like, how does anyone afford gas out here? And Ginny says it's impossible to find a halfway decent job."

"Ginny?"

"Fabi's girlfriend."

I was about to ask who Fabi was when I remembered she was one of the roommates. At least, I was pretty sure.

"I got one audition, and it was for an extra. In a *commercial.* An extra in a commercial. That's fucking worthless. And I only got the audition because Fabi's dad has connections."

"Everyone has to start somewhere," I couldn't resist pointing out. "An audition, and you've only lived there for two days? That's amazing."

"But a commercial?" she scoffed.

"Remember what we talked about this summer? It won't happen overnight. Just like me fixing up this house. You have to lay the foundation first and then build on it."

"You're not literally laying foundations though, right? Or is it really that bad?"

"No, not quite that bad. Metaphorical foundations."

"I guess so."

"One audition will lead to another, and another, and another. You'll meet people. Make connections. How could they forget a unique face like yours? And your name? Chloe Callaway – it's like you were born to be an actor."

I could sense her smile through the phone.

"Yeah, yeah," she said sheepishly, but I could tell she was mollified.

"Besides, you've got a graphic design degree, so maybe you could use that in the meantime."

"Ugh, I'm so over graphic design. It's not fun anymore."

"This isn't about fun; it's about being able to afford food."

"Whatever, Mom."

"Chloe..."

"Look, when I talk to you, I don't need you to say stuff like that. I just need you to be like, 'yay, you're going to be so famous'!"

"Chloe."

"Fine. If I'm ever on the brink of poverty, I'll look for a graphic design job."

"Good. So, are you ever going to send me pictures of your apartment?"

"You could just come visit and see it for yourself," she suggested hopefully.

"I promise I will, as soon as I can."

"Also, I put a couple of pictures on Instagram, but I guess you deleted your account?"

"Oh, yeah, I did. It had too many pictures of me and Daniel. It was easier to get rid of it all."

"Mm. Maybe you should start a new one. You could post house progress pics! You'd be like some outdoorsy lumber-babe DIY goddess."

"Maybe."

"Anyway, I should go. These job applications aren't going to fill themselves out."

She made a dramatic retching noise, I laughed, and the call ended.

<hr>

AFTER SHOVELING DOWN THE stone-cold, tongue-numbingly spicy Thai noodles, I re-heated my mocha over the fire and set to work unloading the truck. Then I realized I didn't have a good place to store my supplies, which led me to the free-standing garage. The realtor had left me a key to the padlock, but I hadn't used it yet. Once again, I was struck by how little thought I'd put into purchasing this house. It was very unlike Indiana Michelle.

When I opened the garage, a horrendous smell almost made the noodles come back up. Monster rushed forward to investigate the new space but stopped short at the brink, tail and nose drooping. My own nose felt like it had been stuffed with rotting squirrels.

"Jesus Christ," I said, backing away a few feet, eyes watering.

Much as I wanted to slam the door shut and never open it again, until the locks on the house were changed, this was the most secure place for my tools and expensive lumber, not to mention the table saw. So, I pulled on a pair of elbow-high rubber gloves, donned my heavy-duty P100 respirator, and entered.

I had been expecting piles of junk and mountains of garbage and a few rodent corpses, but there was surprisingly little inside. An old dresser with all its drawers missing sagged in the corner, undoubtedly musty with rot, but not bad enough to be the source of the smell. A tarnished gold birdcage and what appeared to be a bird perch sat together. The bottom of the cage was scraped up, making me think of the scratches in the upstairs bedroom.

A bird, I realized. *Those marks came from bird talons.*

There were a few moldy boxes, but even they didn't seem to be causing the terrible smell. I had searched the entire garage and still had no clue what reeked.

Needing a break (and some clean air), I retreated to the river, sitting on the rocky bank with my legs stretched out in front of me. Monster, who had abandoned me at the garage, slunk over looking ashamed.

"Don't worry about it," I told him. "Your sense of smell is a thousand times better than mine, so I can only imagine how awful it was for you."

He licked my hand affectionately as I watched a yellow leaf navigate the choppy gray water and pondered what to do next.

Back in Indiana, back when I was married, I would've asked Daniel to take care of the garage or at least call someone to take care of it. Not that I was overly dependent on him, but our lives had been entwined since high school, and getting his help was as natural and compulsive as yawning. He cooked dinner and killed bugs and dealt with the internet company. I folded laundry, tripped the breakers, and unblocked the garbage disposal. Our respective routines and responsibilities happened without thought. It was taking time and effort to make myself remember that here, nobody would help me; if I didn't complete a task, it wouldn't get done.

"Wish me luck," I said a few minutes later, getting to my feet. "If I'm not back in an hour, run and get Lester."

Monster grunted in a way that told me he remembered exactly who Lester was and had zero intention of going to him for help, even if I passed out from the stench.

Not wanting to contaminate Chloe's jeans, I changed into an older, rattier pair and one of my dad's old charity 5K t-shirts. Since I couldn't pinpoint the source of the smell, maybe giving the whole garage a good scrub would do the trick. Strapping on the respirator once more, I returned to the garage and got to work.

The moldy boxes were tossed unceremoniously outside (*note to self: check on trash service*), and the drawer-less dresser was broken down with a sledgehammer, which was oddly satisfying. I kept the birdcage and perch, though I wasn't sure why. They had a kind of rustic appeal and could easily be cleaned up.

Once the garage was empty, I pulled aside the respirator and sniffed tentatively.

"Oh god," I said, clamping it back over my face. "Nope."

It was getting dark out, so I set up the two portable lights I'd bought, pointing them directly into the garage, thinking I must have missed something obvious. But I didn't see anything, aside from the cracked concrete floor and the slightly warped wooden walls. For a moment, I debated calling my mom to get her opinion. She was the cleaning queen, with a solution for every smell and stain. But I was afraid she'd want to see pictures, and then she would think I was living in filth and poverty and tell me to come home, and I would be tempted to.

I hadn't bought a lot of cleaning supplies yet, figuring that a deep clean would be one of the final steps in my process, but I at least had a bottle of all-purpose cleaner and many rags. With a ratty old broom I found, I swept the cobwebs and dead bugs out of the corners. Then, on hands and knees, I scrubbed. The floor didn't look particularly grimy, but maybe something nasty had soaked in a long time ago and refused to leave.

As I worked, the sky got darker and darker. At one point, Monster settled beside the truck, close enough to keep an eye on me but far enough not to be overwhelmed by the stench. It was tedious work, and I wished I hadn't forgotten my headphones in Indiana and then forgotten to buy a new pair today.

"One list ends and another begins," I said, my voice muffled. It was one of my mom's most-used phrases, usually pertaining to grocery lists.

In the center of the floor, my rag snagged on a crack and got stuck. When I tugged it loose, a chunk of concrete came with it, as well as a thin, ivory-colored fragment that I thought was ceramic. Inspecting it more closely, I saw that it was curved, and the inside was tinged with dark brown.

Part of me understood right away what it was, though the knowledge took a while to penetrate.

"What the fuck."

I turned to the spot in the floor where the piece of concrete had popped out. There were other loose pieces, and I pried one free, knowing I shouldn't, but unable to stop. The old concrete crumbled between my fingers, falling with a soft patter. Mixed into it were more of the ivory fragments that I was now certain were bones.

CHAPTER 6

MONSTER'S BARKS BOOMED FROM inside the house where I'd locked him up while the forensics team went in and out of the garage. They had been there for an hour and a half already, breaking up the floor and placing bone fragments in plastic evidence bags. Two police officers stood nearby, conversing in low voices. The young male officer – Hodgkins or Hopkins or something – shot me frequent glances.

Maybe he thinks I'm hot, I mused. *Or maybe he thinks I'm nuts.*

To be fair, I had sounded nuts on the phone. Like an idiot, I had once again forgotten the address, so while I explained that I had just moved in a few days ago, I frantically tore through the pages in the realtor's packet.

"214 New Hampshire Route 58," I said at last, practically laughing with relief.

Maybe I should've noted the long pause on the other end. Maybe I should've realized how strange it was when the forensics team showed up without the police having first confirmed that there were actually bones. Honestly, I was just glad they believed me, because I could hardly believe it myself.

A new car rolled down the crowded driveway and stopped beside my truck. Even from a distance, I could tell that the man who got out was tired. His shoulders slumped, and he walked in an ambling, bored way.

"Over here," called Hodges, raising a hand.

The new arrival conferred with the officers for a few minutes, poked his head into the garage to converse with the forensics team, and then headed my way. Every muscle in my body clenched as he approached.

"I'm Detective Engstrom," said the tired man, flashing his badge. His eyes were permanently half-closed. "Callum PD, cold cases division."

"Callum?" I said nervously. "Isn't that kind of far away?"

"Walk me through what happened," he said, not deigning to answer my question.

I repeated the story I'd already told the officers and the lead forensic – that I'd been cleaning the floor when I dislodged a chunk of concrete and noticed the bone fragment in it. He listened with no apparent interest, though I thought I saw a shadow cross his face when I mentioned the birdcage in passing.

"What were you doing cleaning the floor so late at night?" he asked.

"Um." Words escaped me for a moment. "I... I was trying to get rid of the smell."

"The smell. What smell?"

"In the garage? It's pretty terrible."

He stared at me until I started to second-guess myself. But he'd been in the garage, so surely, he'd smelled it. Detective Engstrom clicked his pen and jotted something in his small, spiral-bound notebook.

"How did you know the bones were human?"

My eyes widened. "Excuse me?"

"You must know a lot about bones to be able to tell they're human from such small pieces."

"I didn't know. Seriously, I thought... I thought they were from an animal."

"Why would you call the police over animal bones?"

"I meant to say that I wasn't sure what they were from."

"Can you provide proof of ownership?"

"Ownership of what?"

"This house. I was under the impression it's been empty since the 80s."

Flustered, I handed him the paperwork that I had been clutching ever since calling 911. Then I showed him my driver's license.

"Indiana," he said. "What made you move all the way out here?"

"Divorce," I said, and immediately regretted it.

"We're all done here!" called one of the forensic techs, waving an arm. "Packing up."

"If you find anything else," said Detective Engstrom, handing me a card, "call me."

"Wait!" I said as he turned to leave. "Are you telling me there might be more bones? Or bodies?"

"I'm not at liberty to discuss open cases."

"But you said you work cold cases, right?"

That shadow again, and then a flicker of what might've been a smile. "This case has been reopened."

<hr>

NEVER BEFORE HAD I longed so much for internet access. That night, which I spent inside the house again, I tried using my phone to search for cold cases in New Hampshire, but it was so slow to load that I gave up after ten minutes. If Spencer had known anything weird about this house, surely he would've tried harder to talk me out of buying it. Still, I would text him in the morning.

I also debated texting Chloe, since it was still only 9:00 PM in LA. Then I remembered how much she hated true crime documentaries and podcasts, always saying that they made her paranoid and jumpy.

"Once that shit is in my head, I'll never be able to get it out," she told me.

If she knew that I was *living* in a true crime documentary, she would definitely freak out.

The whole experience – the bones, the cops, the forensic team in their coveralls and plastic booties, Detective Engstrom and his million questions – already felt like a dream. I wished it *had* been a dream, thrilling and exciting and fun to tell people about but ultimately not real.

It is *real, though. It's real. It happened. There was a body under my garage floor. A human body.*

Had the previous owner of the house hidden it there? Or perhaps... a close neighbor? Was Lester a retired serial killer? Or worse, an active one?

"Now who's being paranoid," I muttered, setting down my phone and pinching the bridge of my nose.

When I finally fell asleep, I dreamed about the house again. The dream started exactly as it had before, with me walking down a tree-lined road, though this time I also passed over a covered bridge. Then I saw the A-frame. It was crumbling into pieces, and I hurried toward it, my feet unsteady on the gravel drive. The front door collapsed at my touch. Strangely enough, the inside of the house was perfectly fine. More than fine – fixed and fully furnished, like I'd stepped through a portal and ended up in the 1960s, when it was built. In the middle of the hall was the golden bird perch, and resting on it was a dark shape. Wanting to know what it was, I moved closer, reaching my hand out to see if it had feathers or fur. Before I could touch it, its skin slipped away, falling to the floor, revealing cracked bones that remained upright on the perch.

When I woke, I was certain that I was being watched. Remaining very still, I looked out the glass wall, half-expecting to see Lester standing on the back deck. But all I could see were the silhouettes of trees against the soft gray of early dawn.

I glanced up at the hole in the ceiling just in time to see a dark shape flutter away.

My phone buzzed, making me jump and Monster's ears twitch. It wasn't a text – it was a reminder notification for Daniel's birthday. In an attempt to be friendly, I could've sent him a Happy Birthday message and asked what his plans were for the day, but his plans would undoubtedly be the same as they always were: take a half day off work, go to the movie theater by himself to see some stupid action movie, then go out with friends and drink way too much. The only thing that might be different now that I was gone was the sloppy, intoxicated birthday sex.

Actually, that might happen anyway, just with a different woman.

That thought made my insides curl. I reminded myself that I was the one who had wanted a divorce, that I was happy about the divorce, that I would've snapped if I'd had to stay in that house with him one second longer, that I'd never liked the sloppy birthday sex, anyway.

Thank god I'd deleted social media, or I would've been tempted to spy on him.

"Redirect," I said, putting the phone away. "You have a thousand things to get done today."

The phone was back in my hands a minute later, though, as I vaguely recalled that I had planned to text Spencer about something. What had it been? My fingers hovered indecisively over the screen.

"Oh, well. It must not have been important."

FALLING WAS A LEGITIMATE concern given the steep slope of the A-frame roof. But I had installed brackets and toe boards, and the work needed to be done, so I made a point of moving slowly and steadily and did my best not to look down.

"Maintain three points of contact," I reminded myself constantly, recalling what I'd read in my research. "Foot, foot, hand."

The nails in the shingles were so rusted that I had to put all my weight behind the pry bar in order to pull them up. The bucket I'd brought with me was soon full, and it took several trips down the anchored ladder to empty it before I was done. Beneath the old shingles was stiff, crumbling plastic sheeting, which I tossed over the side, watching it flop down into the yard.

Patching up the hole was a trickier process, involving my circular saw, plywood, and tar paper. My arms trembled with the effort, but the longer I was up there, the less I feared falling. Once the tar paper was secured, there wasn't much I could do until the new shingles were delivered, so I ate a quick sandwich and set out to explore the parts of the property I hadn't seen much of yet. Rather than turn south toward Lester's house, I turned north.

The trail that the realtor had so proudly mentioned was nothing more than shallow steps carved into an incline, so covered in pine needles that I'd nearly missed them.

"Come on, Monster," I said as I placed each foot carefully. I'd been on the roof for so long that the ground actually seemed less stable now.

He raced past me, not even using the steps. I had a strange sense of déjà vu as I followed, though I wasn't sure why until I saw the hole. Pale green lichen mottled the boulder, at the base of which the hole gaped, big enough for a child to crawl into. Monster stared intently into its depths, growling low and constant. I remembered him doing the exact same thing on the night we camped out, when I woke up and couldn't find him. That night felt like it had been years ago, though it had only been a few days.

"Dear god, please don't let there be any bones down there," I said.

Kneeling and taking a deep breath, I turned on my phone's flashlight and peered into the hole. There weren't any bones that I could see, but there was a scattering of brown and gray feathers.

When I reached toward the hole, Monster let out a yip.

"Geez, calm down. It's a hole, buddy. They happen some-times..."

I trailed off as I realized I had said those exact words last time. The sensation that my life was an endless loop washed over me, but I shook it off. This was nothing compared to the loop my life used to be – wake up at 6, go for a walk, go to work, home by 7, eat dinner, watch a few episodes of a sitcom, shower, bed. Every. Single. Day. For close to a decade.

And yet, what was so bad about stability?

Not stability. Monotony.

Chloe and I had talked about that a lot over the summer – how we both dreaded change. But we also figured out that we both couldn't stand the idea of things staying the same for the rest of our lives – the same routine, the same people, the same unfulfilled yearning for something we couldn't quite define.

"You've already cut the big tie," she had said, making a snip-ping motion with her fingers. "If you're brave enough to change that, you're brave enough to change anything."

Of course, I hadn't told her the real reason for the divorce. That was the kind of thing that no big sister would ever want to admit to her little sister.

CHAPTER 7

A LIGHT DRIZZLE WAS falling, meaning no more work on the outside of the house that day. Too much risk of slipping. This time, Monster didn't need as much persuading to leave the hole. He slunk along at my heels, his ears flat against his head and his tail limp. Whatever had made its home in that hole, Monster was not a fan.

Before we went inside, I paused to look at the garage. No caution tape criss-crossed the door, and no crime scene debris littered the area. If I hadn't been there to witness what happened, I would've had no clue. Unfortunately, though, I hadn't been officially cleared to re-enter the garage or put my supplies in it. The table saw was still on my porch, covered in a plastic tarp.

Digging in my pocket, I removed Detective Engstrom's card. One of the corners was bent, and I couldn't stop messing with it as I stepped into the house and pressed my phone to my ear.

"Engstrom," said a bored voice.

"Hi, um, this is Michelle Callaway. From the house? Last night?"

"What can I do for you, Miss Callaway?"

"Are the forensics people all done with my garage? Am I allowed to go back inside?"

"Hold on."

There was a muffled conversation in the background. Just then, through the storm door, I spotted Lester at the edge of the woods. He raised a gnarled hand in greeting, and I smiled in return, pointing at the phone to indicate I was busy.

"Miss Callaway?"

"Yes, I'm here."

"I'm afraid the team will need to come out a second time for further excavation."

"Okay," I said slowly. "I kind of need that garage for storage?"

"You were going to lay a new foundation anyway, right? Think of it as us doing you a favor by getting rid of the old one."

"What am I supposed to do in the meantime?"

He sighed. "The department will arrange for a temporary storage shed. Will that do?"

"I guess. I mean yes, thank you. But why do they need to keep searching? Do they think there's another" – I glanced at Lester and lowered my voice, even though a door and quite some space separated us – "body? Or bodies?"

"You know I can't answer that."

"But it's my property. Can't you tell me anything?"

"We'll be in touch regarding the storage shed."

He hung up. I shoved the phone and the business card into my pocket.

"Sorry about that," I said, stepping back outside but remaining on the porch.

"That was quite a to-do last night," said Lester, edging around Monster. "I could see the lights all the way from my house."

"I hope they didn't keep you up."

"Nah, I don't sleep much anyway these days. Part of getting old."

We stood there awkwardly for a moment until I figured out that he wasn't here just to chit-chat.

"The police were here," I said. "They were searching the garage."

One of Lester's crazily bushy white eyebrows rose. "Been here less than a week and you're already in trouble with the law?"

"No, not yet." I hesitated, but what was the harm in telling him the truth? "Actually, I found bones when I was cleaning the floor. Human bones, according to the detective. They wouldn't really tell me anything, but my best guess is that the foundation was poured over..."

I trailed off. The paper-thin skin of Lester's wrinkled face had gone stark white. He looked like he might cross over to the other side at any moment. I slid my hand into my pocket and touched my phone, ready to call for an ambulance, and I said his name a few times with no response. Just as I was about to dial 911, he muttered:

"Up, down, up, down. Left, right, left, right."

They were the same words I'd heard that first night, when I'd accidentally spied on him from the trees, and they didn't make any more sense now than they had then. Wasn't word repetition like this a sign of stroke?

"What does that mean? Lester?"

"I have to go home now," said Lester suddenly.

And with that, he was gone, tromping off through the woods. Totally nonplussed, I watched until he was out of sight. My phone vibrated a few minutes later, but the noise barely penetrated my bewildered brain. I blinked rapidly, swallowed hard, and forced myself to focus on the text from Spencer. Just seeing his name on the screen made me feel like I was forgetting something, like I'd meant to message him earlier, but I couldn't remember why.

S: Hey, if you're not too busy, I'm having friends over for dinner tonight. You should join us!

S: I understand if you're not in the mood though.

The idea of socializing was unappealing, but I thought back to what I'd told Chloe the day before: *"You have to lay the foundations first and then build on them."* I had been talking about her career and about the house, but I supposed the same logic applied to making friends. Without friends, New Hampshire would never feel like home. And without awkward dinners like this, I would never make friends. Where else would I meet people? In the woods?

M: Can I bring Monster?
S: I'm offended you even need to ask.
M: Lol. What time?

ALTHOUGH IT WAS A Monday night, and this dinner was in no way a party, the urge to dress nicely compelled me to dump all my clothes on the not-so-clean floor and sort through every single item. Would these native New Hampshirites mock me for bundling up on a night that wasn't even supposed to drop below fifty degrees? I decided I didn't care. I hadn't adapted yet, and I needed warmth.

In the end, I wore nice black leggings, gray boots, and a soft gray sweater. I even left my hair down and put on a necklace, a long silver chain with a coiled snake pendant, given to me by my best friend in high school. I hadn't worn any jewelry since giving my wedding and engagement rings back to Daniel to do with as he pleased.

My reflection in the glass wall was not entirely awful, though the necklace looked a tad juvenile. *Good enough*, I thought, pulling on my coat and attaching Monster's leash to his harness.

Spencer's house was in the opposite direction from Arden Woods, closer to a town called Paloma. It wasn't as isolated as my property, but it was set far back from the road. The driveway continued for so long that I started to think I'd taken a wrong turn, even though I'd lived there for three weeks after I moved. Then, I caught a flash of light through the trees.

The house was a classic Cape Cod with a spacious front porch, which was criss-crossed with strands of warm white lights. On the night I arrived in New Hampshire, Spencer and I had sat on that porch under those lights drinking decaf coffee and reminiscing about college while Monster lounged at our feet. Spencer had made me laugh and forget all about Chloe driving cross-country to LA all by herself in what she described as "a three-week wandering journey with a sunny destination".

Three cars were already parked out front. I pulled up behind them while Monster danced in his seat, letting out low, excited groans.

"You have to chill, okay?" I said. "Don't scare away my potential new friends."

He tilted his head as if to say: *How could I possibly scare anyone? I'm the cutest good boy on the planet.*

"I know." I let out a sigh. "Okay, let's go."

As I was about to let myself in through the front door, laughter sounded from the backyard. Monster strained against his leash, and since he weighed almost as much as I did, I had no choice but to follow. Soon, a blazing fire pit came into view. Four figures were seated around it, and they looked up when Monster barked.

"Hey!" called Spencer. "Glad you made it!"

"Oh my god," said a familiar voice. "Look at that beast."

One of the figures approached, and I immediately recognized the curly hair.

"Hannah?" I asked.

"Hi again." She didn't seem at all surprised to see me. "This must be Monster."

Squatting, she scratched his ears ferociously, giggling when he licked her cheek. Then, the three of us made our way over to the fire.

You can do this, I told myself. *Just don't be weird.*

"I didn't know you and Hannah were friends," I said to Spencer.

"Best friends," Hannah corrected. "Us poor nerds had to stick together in high school."

"Come on, it wasn't that bad," said a woman with sleek red hair. "Nobody persecuted us."

"Yeah, but they didn't want to hang out with us either," said Spencer.

"Speak for yourself," said a man with an impressive black beard. "I was very popular."

"Only because you're rich," said Hannah, kicking him playfully. "And straight."

"True. I'm Reuben, by the way," he said smoothly, shaking my hand.

The others groaned and rolled their eyes, and I couldn't help smiling. So far, they seemed like a pretty nice group, though not the group I would've been friends with in high school. I hadn't really *had* a group in high school, come to think of it, at least until I met Daniel.

"I'm Francesca," said the redhead with a nod in my direction. "Nice to meet you."

"Nice to meet you all, too. I'm Michelle. Oh, and this is Monster."

He had been getting pets and scratches this whole time, and now he became the center of attention for a couple of minutes. They asked what breed he was (Bernese mountain dog), where I'd gotten him (rescued from a drainage ditch), and how much he weighed (a whopping 110). Not only a nice group, but a group of dog-lovers. Daniel had never liked dogs, or any animals for that matter. During the year and a half of our marriage that had overlapped with owning Monster, Daniel had never once touched him.

"We're not keeping that dog," he'd said when I'd come home with a dirty, malnourished puppy that I could barely carry. "Just how big is it supposed to get? It's already monstrous."

Thus the name – Monster.

"So," said Spencer, clapping his hands together, "who's hungry?"

We ate burgers – my first genuinely hot food in over a week – and chips. The others drank beer, and I tried to be casual in the way that I declined one. Thankfully, nobody pressed the matter. My contributions to the conversation were minimal, which was fine by me. Francesca apologized for not bringing her wife, Celeste, who was apparently visiting her parents in New York City. Spencer told a story about one of his middle school pupils who had turned to him for advice on coming out. Reuben, who worked on his family's farm, continued to flirt with me in a harmless, definitely-not-serious way.

The four friends were so relaxed and easy with each other. I hadn't had a close friend in years other than Chloe, and sisters weren't the same as friends, no matter how well you got along.

Eventually, I was asked about my job (none), my hobbies (hiking, I guess?), and my family (big, loving, and too far away). Compared to them, I felt boring, and though I was having a decent time, I felt like I didn't truly belong.

It had felt that way in Indiana, too, even with people I'd known for years. At a party not long before my 33rd birthday this past January, I had looked around the room and suddenly thought: *What am I doing here? Who are these people?* Each face was weird and unfamiliar, even my husband's. It had struck me that I hated the parties, hated the people, hated being there. I had only kept going to them because that was what we did. Once I finally accepted that I didn't have to do that anymore, it made the divorce and the migration inevitable.

How long would it take for me to feel at-home here, especially when I had so many ties to other places and other people?

Could this place ever become my true home when my heart was elsewhere?

"Can I walk you to your car?" Hannah asked a couple of hours later when I declared that it was time to head home. "I'm not ready to say goodbye to this sweetheart yet," she explained, ruffling Monster's ears.

"You really love dogs, huh?"

"The bigger and goofier, the better."

"Does your dad's store have any dog beds? I promised Monster a new one."

"Absolutely. But it's not my dad's store anymore, it's mine."

"Wow, really? That's awesome."

"Yeah," she said, not meeting my gaze. "So anyway, did you ever figure out your address?"

"214 New Hampshire Route 58," I recited, choosing not to reveal the incident that had forced me to re-learn it.

"You're kidding, right?"

"No," I said, noting her strange expression. "Why?"

"Didn't Spencer tell you? Actually, now that I think about it, he might not know."

"Know what?"

We came to a stop beside my truck. Without the fire, cold settled in my bones once more, and I wished I'd brought a heavier coat.

"That house," Hannah continued, leaning against the cab and crossing her arms over her chest. "It's the A-frame, right? By the river?"

"Uh huh."

"My dad told me about the lady who lived there in the 60s, right after it was built. He was a kid then, but his dad, my grandpa, had to ban her from the hardware store."

"How come?"

"For starters, they thought she was running an illegal exotic pet trade."

"Seriously?" I asked, half laughing. "That's bizarre."

"Yeah, she kept buying cages and kennels, and she nearly assaulted my grandma when she told her they wouldn't order exotic bird seed."

"This doesn't seem like the most lucrative area for that type of, um, enterprise."

"It's kind of perfect, actually," said Hannah, looking out over the dark treetops. "Out here, people mind their own business. There's lots of space. Neighbors far enough apart that they wouldn't hear anything. And it's only a few hours' drive from several big cities."

"That makes sense," I said, thinking of the scratches on the door and the birdcage in the garage.

"Grandpa told me there was a rumor that she was breeding dragon birds," Hannah continued as she absentmindedly stroked Monster's back.

"Dragon birds?"

"Great eared nightjars. You should look up a picture; they have these long tails and weird heads that are freakishly dragon-like."

"I think I've seen one of those in the woods," I said, recalling the dark shape with the oddly boxy head, the one I hadn't been able to label as either a bird or a bat. "By my house."

"I doubt it."

"What do you mean?"

Hannah shifted slightly. "She only ever managed to get one of them, and it was long dead when the police found it. According to Grandpa, it had been buried under a tree near the house."

"Was it named Simon, by chance?"

The question slipped out, and Hannah gave me a weird look. "I don't know," she said. "I could ask my dad."

"That's okay," I said hastily. "It doesn't matter."

The conversation petered out, leaving an awkward silence. At least, *I* thought it was awkward. Hannah appeared perfectly content to lean against my truck and scratch Monster's ears.

"We should get going," I said. "I'm pretty tired. I haven't been sleeping well."

Way to overshare, Michelle.

"Sounds like you have a caffeine deficiency," Hannah said seriously.

"I definitely do."

"Have you been to Beans & Brews yet?"

"Once. It was really good."

"Next time you stop by the store, we should go over there and start fixing that deficiency."

CHAPTER 8

THAT NIGHT, AS I tried to fall asleep, I watched for the dragon bird through the glass wall. Despite Hannah's certainty that the bird was dead, I was positive I had seen it. Maybe the old owner had imported more nightjars than the authorities were aware of, and maybe they had long lifespans like parrots.

Relentless rain obscured the trees and swelled the river for three whole days, ruining my hopes of finishing the roof. My only consolation was that I had at least patched up the hole and laid more plastic, meaning I didn't have to worry about leaks.

During those rainy days, I made phone calls to utility companies and heard at least three variations of:

"Let me look up that address. Oh my, it appears that this house hasn't been functional since the early 80s, we'll need to send a technician out there to evaluate, and unfortunately we are fully booked until next week."

I made the appointments, keeping meticulous notes of dates and times, then jotted down everything I wanted to get done before then, though I had little motivation to do any of it. One dreary morning, with every good intention, I laid out the materials I would need to work on the kitchen and re-checked my list.

1. *Sand, paint, and seal cabinets*

2. *Pipes under sink*

3. *Connections for stove and oven*

4. *Replace countertops*

5. *Install tile floor*

6. *Order new appliances*

7. *Install stove, vent hood, oven, sink*

My throat tightened. Suddenly, the idea of doing any of it sounded like the worst thing in the world. Though I told myself it was just because I hadn't had any caffeine that morning, I knew it was a deeper problem. I couldn't do this.

Halfway through making a sandwich, I realized I had no appetite for it. Since I had only spread peanut butter so far, I gave it to Monster. Gently, he took it from my hand, carried it to what had become "his" corner, laid down, and ate noisily. Meanwhile, I retreated to my makeshift pillow-bed, pulled out my phone, and was about to text Chloe when I recalled the time difference. There was no way she'd be awake at 7.

I knew I was being stupid and wasting time. Winter was fast approaching, and this house wouldn't magically fix itself. I had chosen to take on this project, and I *wanted* to do it, so why couldn't I make myself do it?

The next time I picked up my phone, I was certain the clock was wrong. It definitely couldn't be 5:45 in the afternoon. Just a minute ago, it hadn't even been noon! But there was an email with a 5:01 timestamp. An entire day wasted. I sent Chloe a text and opened the email, which was from an unfamiliar address: ldean@fletcherwarren.com.

Hey girl, is everything okay? You never responded to my last email. I know you're just in the woods or something and have terrible reception, but shoot me an email when you get a chance so I know you haven't been eaten by a bear or a wolf.

Speaking of wolves...

Daniel called the office again yesterday, my direct line. He asked for your new address, and he said you must have changed your cell number because he couldn't reach you. I told him to give you space.

Stay safe up there...

XO, Lauren

"Lauren," I said. "Duh."

Looking at the email address again, I didn't know how I'd missed the "fletcherwarren" part. That was the name of the firm I had worked at with Lauren – Fletcher & Warren Architects. For nine years, my own email address had been mcallaway@fletcherwarren.com. I had kept my last name after marriage, so the email hadn't even changed then.

What was Daniel playing at, making up lies to try to get my address? I had never asked him to send me anything. When I moved out, I had taken as much as I could to my parents' house, only making one trip back right before the drive to New Hampshire. Hence Monster's missing bed. Could it be that Daniel's lies were an attempt to find out where I was so he could come see me?

Rage bubbled up inside at the idea of him showing up here, in this place that was my new home, my safe haven. Our divorce hadn't been dramatic or contentious. I didn't hate him. But he would cross this threshold over my dead body.

———— ◆ ————

MY ANGER AND CONFUSION over Daniel finally prompted me to get up and get some work done. By the time this new wave of energy ebbed, it was nearly midnight, and the kitchen was a quarter of the way finished. The cabinets were sanded and primed for paint, which I would buy next time I was in Arden Woods. The terrible linoleum countertops had been torn out, and the surfaces prepped for the new granite countertops that I planned to buy. The old, rusted sink had been dumped outside, and the new pipes I'd installed were ready for a far superior stainless steel sink.

Standing back to admire my work, I was a little underwhelmed. It was an island of progress in a big, messy sea. Even so, I was proud of myself for actually doing something.

Chloe hadn't responded to my earlier text, so I sent her another one.

M: What color should I paint my kitchen?
C: Glittery pink, duh
M: No, seriously! You're so much better at color stuff than I am.
C: Send a pic?

Repositioning one of my portable lights, I snapped a picture of the kitchen, careful not to include any other parts of the house.

C: Hmm.
C: What are the counters going to be?
M: Dark gray granite.
C: You need a lighter color for the walls and cabinets to balance it out
C: What about feather gray walls and off-white cabinets?
M: Sounds nice!
C: I could look at some color samples tomorrow and send you specifics if you want
M: Yes please, I'm awful at this stuff. I can fix it, but I can't make it look pretty. I want this house to be the epitome of cozy.
C: I wish I could shop with you!
M: Me too.

C: By the way, I've started posting a lot more on Instagram, kind of my journey in LA

C: You should start a new account and follow me

M: Okay!

Much as I hated the idea, I couldn't really say no. I wasted half an hour picking a username, trying various clever combinations and finally going with "@lumberbabe" because I knew it would make Chloe laugh and because I didn't want to use anything related to my real name.

Then, because I was still too wired to sleep, it was time to get into the loft.

For the past few days, I had been mulling it over, and I had opted to continue with my plan of breaking through the wall on the second story. The idea was to open up the entire floor and make it one big space instead of two bedrooms and the loft. It would become my bedroom, library, etc., and the downstairs bedroom would be for guests, if I ever had any.

As I climbed the stairs, I ripped up the ugly, threadbare carpet runner, tossing it over the railing when I reached the top. Monster immediately started sniffing it.

"Stay down there," I told him. "It's about to be very loud."

With ear plugs in and safety goggles on, I tightened my grip on the sledgehammer and swung it hard. Once, twice, thrice. I had expected the old wood to give way immediately, but it was stronger than expected. A pool of sweat formed on my lower back. I swung again.

Vibrations pinged through my skull at the resounding crack. For a wild moment, I thought the house would collapse on top of me, just like I always feared it would in my dreams. I stood perfectly still, even holding my breath, until I was sure it was okay.

The resultant hole in the wall was barely big enough to fit my arm through, and strangely, I couldn't see into the loft on the other side. I had purposely placed a light in the living room so that when I broke through up here, I wouldn't be totally blind. But the darkness on the other side of the hole was absolute.

Reaching my arm inside, I felt around, thinking that maybe it was some sort of wall cavity used for insulation. My gloved fingers touched emptiness. The space back there had to be at least three or four feet deep. When my hand brushed the opposite wall, I jumped. On that side, it wasn't wood. It was almost like padding.

Half a dozen swings later, the hole was big enough for me to squeeze through, and I did so, shining a light on the floor to make sure it wasn't just insulation. The beam illuminated feathers, fur clumps, and dry animal droppings.

I hesitated, debating whether I should call Detective Engstrom even though it was the middle of the night. Deciding to call him only if I found more bones, I put one leg through and then the other. It was a tight fit, and I was thankful for once in my life for my flat chest.

By my estimation, the space was four feet wide and eight feet long. Since it was at the top of the house, the roof was steeply sloped on either side and high in the center. As I had suspected, the walls were heavily padded with a material that had once been white.

Sound-proofing, I realized with a shudder. *This must be where she kept the illegal exotic animals anytime the police came knocking.*

Precarious piles of rusted cages teetered over rows of scratches on the wooden floor. Holes had been gnawed into the padding in various spots close to the ground. A small, padded door in one wall must have led into the bedroom with all the locks. It was the only way in or out of this hidden room.

I didn't realize my hands were trembling until I dropped the flashlight and it rolled, beam spinning, finally coming to a stop focused on a small mattress crammed into the corner. Reddish stains dotted its mildewed surface.

Okay, so maybe she kept more than animals in here.

At the point where the mattress met the downward slope of the A-frame, there were more scratches on the low ceiling. It took me a moment to realize that they weren't just random – they were jagged words.

Simon is the devil's eyes
Simon turns them all to lies
Simon seeks the world above
Simon takes the ones you love

———◆———

"Wʜᴀᴛ ᴅᴏᴇs ᴛʜᴀᴛ ᴇᴠᴇɴ mean?"

Across from me, Hannah shrugged, wide-eyed.

It had been two days since I'd found the hidden soundproof room. I had returned to the hardware store for more nails and sanding pads, and now Hannah and I were at Beans & Brews. On the table, between our steaming cappuccinos, was a slip of paper on which I'd transcribed the bizarre poem I'd found scratched into the ceiling. She had read it through several times, lips moving, and was now slowly stirring sugar into her coffee.

"That's a pretty big coincidence," she said at last, taking a sip that left a ridge of foam on her top lip.

"What is?"

"That name – Simon. Remember what you said at Spencer's house? You asked me if the bird's name was Simon."

"It was only a hunch. I overheard my neighbor saying that name."

"Your neighbor?"

"Lester. He's weird, but harmless…I think."

"How old would you say he is?"

I shrugged. "Seventy-five? Maybe eighty. Why?"

Hannah uncrossed and recrossed her legs, then drank more coffee. She tucked a dark curl behind her ear, and it immediately sprang loose again.

"Okay, I know you told me not to ask my dad," she said. "But I did it anyway. He didn't know if the bird was named Simon, but get this – that lady who ran the exotic pet trade? Shirley Dennis? Her oldest son was named Simon."

"So someone, maybe Shirley, wrote that freaky poem about him?"

"I guess so."

"I wonder if he's still alive," I mused. "Maybe he could explain it all."

"He's not," said Hannah grimly. "That's what I was going to tell you. In 1966, Shirley killed her kids and then herself."

The blood-stained mattress popped into my mind, and a chill ran down my spine. "Really?"

"My dad said that Shirley had three kids – Simon, Sylvia, and Sharon. Anyway, Shirley's ex-husband reported the kids missing when they were supposed to go to his house in New York for the weekend and never showed up. The police found Shirley dead in her backyard with a note in her pocket saying that her kids were gone. Eventually, they found the kids' bodies in a hole mostly hidden by a boulder."

Dead in her backyard. *My* backyard.

"I know that hole. I've seen it. No wonder Monster was freaked out by it. Did the note explain why she killed them?"

"I don't know. My dad didn't really like talking about it, so it was hard to get anything out of him. And he made me swear not to mention it to my grandpa."

"Why didn't anybody tell me about this when I bought the house? Don't they have to disclose stuff like this? Is that why I got it so cheap?"

"I don't know," Hannah said again with a sympathetic half-smile. "It happened so long ago, maybe the realtor didn't even know."

We sat in silence for a while, drinking our coffee, though I had no desire for mine anymore. It was tasteless, and it soured in my stomach. All the time, money, and effort I'd already put into fixing that house, only to find out that three children had been murdered there. Should I cut my losses and move?

"Wait," I said. "What does this have to do with my neighbor? You asked how old he was."

"Oh, right. Well, a couple of other children in the area went missing not long before the Dennis kids were killed, so the police thought maybe Shirley had killed them too. One was a girl named Patricia Engstrom, and the other was an eight-year-old boy named Kent, who had belonged to the neighbor. I was wondering if Kent might have been Lester's son."

"Those other two were never found?"

"Nope."

Lester's reaction to the news about the bones came back to me. His shock, his paleness, his insane muttering, his sudden need to leave. If Kent was his son, and the body had never been found...

"Are you okay?"

I looked up. Hannah's dark brows were knitted with concern. Old Me would've said I was fine, flashed a smile, and shoved everything deep down. That was part of why Old Me had stayed married so many years. She had pretended for so long that her life was fine that she actually believed it. Almost.

"No," I said. "I'm not okay."

"The whole thing is pretty freaky," Hannah agreed.

"You don't know the half of it."

As I related the story about the bones under the garage floor, her already-large eyes widened until I could see white all the way around her irises.

"So basically, I'm screwed," I finished. "This house is cursed."

"You're not screwed," said Hannah so fiercely that I was taken aback. "And if you're that worried about it, I have one more thing to tell you. My dad said that one of the children – the middle one, Sylvia – survived."

"Seriously?"

"Yeah. She may not be in the area anymore, but I bet you could track her down and talk to her, and I know exactly what she'll say – that the house is not cursed."

"I'm not sure that will help."

Hannah leaned forward, resting her elbows on the table. "Look, you told me your whole reason for moving here was to make a new home for yourself. That house saw some seriously messed up shit. It needs new life too, and I think you're the perfect person to create it."

Because I know what it's like to feel alone and damaged beyond all repair.

"It's like an old nest, right?" Hannah continued. "It's dry and brittle and missing pieces. All it needs is some fresh lining."

"Maybe you're right," I said, choosing not to point out that some birds' nests, like those of owls, were made of the feathers, fur, and bones of their prey.

PART TWO: NESTING

<hr>

"I see at intervals the glance of a curious sort of bird through the close-set bars of a cage: a vivid, restless, resolute captive is there; were it but free, it would soar cloud-high."—Jane Eyre

CHAPTER 9

NEAR-FREEZING TEMPERATURES GRIPPED NEW Hampshire in late October. Throughout that whole month, I had worked at top speed to install shingles on the roof, refresh the insulation, and replace the weatherstripping on all the doors. Due to delays and shortages, the electricity and gas weren't set up until a week before Halloween. My new appliances had been waiting, cold and lifeless, in a corner of the living room for two weeks.

On Halloween night, I cooked my first meal in my new home – a hearty lentil stew that would yield many leftovers, crispy pan-fried potatoes, and a loaf of crusty sourdough (not home-made, but still). By no means was I an excellent chef, but the food was warm and filling, and I ate so much that the rest of the evening was spent on the floor in a lethargic state.

Not knowing whether to expect any trick-or-treaters, I had bought a few bags of candy. However, the doorbell didn't ring once, and I knew it was functional because I'd fixed it.

"I'm sorry, buddy," I told Monster, who was moping.

For a while, he had waited excitedly by the door, turning in circles. Then he sat. Then he laid down with his head between his paws. Halloween was his favorite night of the year because he got to meet so many new people and hear their excited squeals over his cuteness. Back in Indiana, the constant promise of the ringing doorbell had kept him on tenterhooks for hours.

Halloween used to be my favorite holiday, too, because it was the one time every year when I stayed home instead of going to a party with Daniel. I drank wine, handed out (and ate) candy, and watched all the Paranormal Activity movies (Daniel hated them).

This year, instead of chomping on chocolate and laughing every time Monster tried to tackle a kid in a Spider-Man costume, I lay on my bed of pillows in a food coma.

Maybe parents can sense that this place is evil, I mused. *Even if they don't know what happened here, they can feel the sinister energy, and they don't want their kids anywhere near it.*

A notification went off on my phone, and I saw that Chloe had posted a new photo on Instagram. Not surprising. She posted at least once a day. Lately, it had been my only way of getting news from her, as her texts and calls got less and less frequent.

"Hey Monster, want to see what Aunt Chloe is up to?"

His mournful puppy-dog eyes clearly said no.

"Suit yourself."

Do you realize that you talk to your dog more than any actual person?

When I opened Instagram and saw Chloe's post, there was a strange moment where I didn't even recognize her. All I saw were three young women posing in short-skirted versions of the Sanderson sisters' costumes from Hocus Pocus. It was actually a well-done photo, and the costumes (other than their shortness) were spot on. I wondered if they were Chloe's roommates.

Then I took a closer look at Sarah Sanderson and realized it was Chloe.

"What did you do to your hair?" I demanded of the screen as if it could answer for her.

Chloe's hair, like mine, was naturally wavy, though hers was a gorgeous honey blonde while mine was a basic light brown.

Now, though, her hair was straight as a pin and platinum blonde. I zoomed in, hoping it was a wig, but it clearly wasn't.

"Is that a septum ring? Yep, it's a septum ring. What the hell."

It just wasn't her style. It wasn't *her*.

My eyes couldn't tear away from the picture. It wasn't only the hair and the nose ring – her face, her demeanor, everything was different, like I was looking at a total stranger.

To make sure I wasn't insane, I scrolled back to a picture from before LA. In it, she and I were squeezed into one hammock, so close our cheeks were nearly touching. Somehow, she had managed to take it at the exact moment we realized how stuck we were. My eyes were squeezed shut, my teeth bared in a wild grin. Her mouth was wide open, mid-laugh.

I let the image sink in, then quickly scrolled back to the Halloween picture. I could see her now – the shape of her eyes, the freckle just to the left of her nose, the faint smile lines. Sighing, I dropped my phone facedown onto the floor.

"Well, at least one of us is adapting."

◆

"DON'T YOU WANT TO see your nieces and nephew? Don't you want to watch the Macy's parade with me? Don't you want to help get the Christmas decorations out of the attic?"

Clearly, my mom had been expecting a fight when she'd called and had prepared a list of ways to guilt me into coming home for Thanksgiving.

"Mom, I—"

"You can't be up there alone on Thanksgiving with nothing but a microwavable frozen meal."

"Hey," I protested. "I can cook."

"And besides," she continued as if I hadn't spoken, "even if you want a home-cooked meal, you don't want to go to all that trouble just for yourself. Wouldn't you rather fly home? We're

having all the old favorites: turkey, ham, green bean casserole, pecan pie. And Christy says she's making a new dessert.
Something..." She paused for dramatic effect. "Chocolatey."

Damn it, Christy.

My sister-in-law was a great baker, though where she found
the time between working as a nurse and dealing with three
kids, I had no idea. Against my will, I imagined choco-
late-hazelnut pie, layered chocolate mousse, gooey chocolate
lava cakes.

"I'm not sure I have the money to fly home," I said. "The
house needs a little more work than I anticipated."

"Your father and I can—"

"No," I said a little too quickly. "That's okay. I'll drive. It's
better for Monster, anyway."

"Do you have enough time to make the drive?"

"Yeah, why wouldn't I?"

"Oh, I thought maybe you'd found a job."

"Not yet."

Truthfully, I hadn't even considered looking for a job. Not
only was I busy getting the house ready for winter, but I
simply had no idea what I wanted to do. Architecture was
the obvious choice, since that's what I'd gotten my degrees
in and had years of experience in. But the idea of going back
to eight-to-five office culture made me want to die.

From a financial standpoint, I had no immediate need for
a job. Daniel and I had always kept separate bank accounts.
It was one of those weird things that didn't make sense at the
time, and he had questioned it at least once a year, but I was
beyond grateful for it now. We had shared everything else, and
we had split all payments equally, but keeping our earnings
in separate accounts always made me more comfortable. So
when we divorced, it was a clean split, financially speaking. I
had lots of savings, and he couldn't fight me for a single penny.

"Is Chloe coming for Thanksgiving?" I asked, hoping to
derail my mom from that line of questioning.

"I haven't asked yet, but I suppose if we pay for a plane ticket, she'll have no objection."

"I suppose."

Her recent lack of communication didn't give me much hope. On the other hand, maybe she would be ready for some cold weather and home-cooked food. I imagined she'd been living off cheese, crackers, and avocados.

After the call with my mom, I plugged my phone in to charge, and Monster and I went for a long walk, trekking all the way past Lester's house toward the distant bridge that spanned the river. I peered through the trees, hoping to catch a glimpse of him, because ever since I had opened my big mouth about the bones, I hadn't heard a peep from him. No luck, though.

If I don't hear from him by the time I leave for Indiana, I'll knock on his door.

That's what neighbors did, right? Checked on each other?

The prospect of going home — why did I still think of it as home? — had filled me with an odd mixture of excitement and dread. It wasn't part of my plan. I still had a ton of work to do on the house and couldn't really afford a break, not with winter breathing down my neck. Spencer and Hannah had both invited me to their family Thanksgivings; surely it would be better for me to stay here and build my foundations.

And yet, it would be nice to sleep in an actual bed and see my family. Even though it had only been a couple of months since I'd seen them all, it felt more like a year. Being all alone in the woods made time stretch.

There was no point in waffling, I decided as Monster and I crossed the bridge over the rapids. I had already told my mom I would come, which was as good as a blood oath.

With the trip to Indiana fast approaching, I worked toward a new deadline: finish the entire downstairs before November 20. That gave me almost three weeks to sand and polish the floors, fix the crack in the glass, and redo the guest bedroom and bathroom, which remained untouched.

When I got back to the house after my walk, I did a quick assessment of all that remained to be done, jotted down a list, and headed to Arden Woods.

"You look focused today," said Hannah when I entered Hayden & Sons.

"I have a lot to get done in the next few weeks. I'm making the trip home – I mean, back to Indiana – for Thanksgiving."

"Oh, so I guess you won't be crashing the Hayden Family Fall Fiasco?"

"Not this year. I appreciate the invite, though."

"That's okay." Hannah shrugged as she started scanning my items. "Part of me didn't want to subject you to that, anyway. It always ends in my dad telling my brothers how disappointed he is that they didn't take over the hardware store, my mom slamming pots and pans around instead of just asking us to help her, and my grandma asking me when I'm getting a boyfriend."

Her cheeks turned a little pink. She kept her eyes on the counter as she put a roll of painter's tape into a paper sack.

"I can only imagine what my grandma will say this year," I said. "I didn't even tell her about the divorce, so she'll be confused when my ex doesn't show up. Honestly, I think she always liked him more than she liked me."

The word "divorce" hung in the air, and I realized that I hadn't mentioned that to Hannah yet. Should I expound on it? Or let the moment pass by?

"Do you need someone to watch Monster while you're gone?" Hannah asked, relieving the tension.

"No, he'll come with me. I'm driving."

"Must be a pretty long drive."

"About 16 hours."

"Wow. Well, maybe when you get back, I can come over and see him. And you, of course. Not that... I mean, you know. I could bring coffee or something."

"That sounds great."

"Hey, didn't you just buy some of these?" She held up a box of nails and shook it gently.

Now that I thought about it, I was pretty sure I had a few unopened boxes of nails sitting on the kitchen counter.

"They're just in case," I said. "Gotta hold that house together somehow."

I paid, loaded up my truck, and was about to leave when I realized I'd left my phone at home on the charger. Normally, it would've been no big deal. I wasn't one of those people who freaked out if my phone wasn't in my hand at all times. But I had been hoping to hear from Chloe once my mom called her about Thanksgiving, because if I knew she was going to be there, I'd be a lot more excited about it.

Eager to check my messages, I drove home a little faster than I should have, sliding a couple of times on invisible ice. Monster was waiting for me in the driveway, tail wagging. This was the first time I'd left him there alone, and I was relieved to know he hadn't wandered off or fixated on that hole again.

Arms full of bags, I shoved through the front door and down the narrow hall to the kitchen. I set everything down and reached for my phone, but it wasn't on the counter.

"Just hold on, okay?" I told Monster, who was eager for attention. "That's right. I plugged the charger in near the boxes."

Sure enough, there it was, but my phone wasn't connected to it. Thinking it might've somehow fallen, I searched all around my still-unpacked boxes and plastic tubs. Then I took apart my pillow bed.

Still nothing.

"Okay," I said, taking a step back. "Remain calm. Even though I'm 99.9% sure that I plugged my phone in before I left, I must have put it somewhere else. If only you were a bloodhound, Monster."

He grinned his stupid, carefree grin, and I couldn't resist burying my face in his thick neck fur. He definitely needed a bath, but I didn't mind. After a year and a half of hearing Daniel complain about Monster being on the couch and getting his fur everywhere and drooling on the kitchen floor, it was nice not to worry about those things.

Very faintly, I heard a buzz. I pulled back from Monster, listening intently. A few seconds later, I heard it again, coming from above.

"Stay," I told Monster when we reached the bottom of the stairs, still not trusting them to hold our weight.

The steps seemed even more unstable than usual. I hadn't been up there since discovering the secret, soundproof room. That place gave me a bad feeling. If evil spirits or vengeful ghosts existed anywhere in this house, they were in that room.

I scanned the landing for my phone, then checked both bedrooms. Standing in the hall, I faced the hole I'd made with my sledgehammer, closed my eyes, and listened, desperately hoping I was wrong.

Thirty seconds passed. A minute. Maybe I *was* wrong.

No sooner had the thought crossed my mind than my phone buzzed once more, the sound clearly coming from inside the hidden room. I could've gone down for a flashlight. I should've. But more than anything, I wanted to get it over with.

The hole seemed smaller than it had been before. As I shoved my way through, my shirt caught on a jagged edge of wood and the fabric tore, hot pain slicing through my upper arm. When I finally made it through, I glanced left, then right. My insides froze. A dark, upright shape lurked in the corner.

At almost the same moment, I spotted a pinprick of light on the floor at my feet. My phone! I had no idea why the flashlight was on, but I didn't have time to figure it out. Snatching it up, I aimed the light into the corner. A second later, I let out a shaky half-laugh, half-sob.

"You fucking idiot."

The ominous shape was nothing more than an old birdcage on top of a stand. Apparently, I couldn't tell the difference between an inanimate object and a human.

"This is the trash can behind the curtain all over again. Moron."

Phone in hand, I climbed back through the hole and took a minute to lean against the wall and attempt to slow my breathing. As the adrenaline rush ebbed, the cut in my arm throbbed, pulsing in time with my racing heartbeat.

Relieved as I was that I'd found my phone, my head was swirling. How had it ended up in that room? Had I gone up there for some reason and just didn't remember? My memory hadn't been great lately, but that was a huge thing to forget. There was no other logical explanation, though.

Then again, maybe the explanation didn't have to be logical.

I thought back to Hannah's reassurance that the house wasn't cursed, but how would she know? She hadn't seen what I'd seen. She hadn't seen the way things moved and changed, the shapes and shadows in the corners of my eyes, the bones in the garage. This had never been her home. She had never lived here.

But there was somebody who *had* lived here.

Moving to the stairs and sitting on the top step, I used my phone to search for "Sylvia Dennis New Hampshire".

There were surprisingly few articles online about the Dennis family's tragedy, especially considering that two missing children had never been found. In the articles I did find, there were old photos of my house that sent shivers up my spine. It looked the same – better, even – yet completely different. Not mine.

One photo captured Shirley Dennis and her three kids posing in front of the back glass wall of the house. Shirley's hair was elegantly curled and pinned, and her clothes gave the appearance of wealth. The children had hair in varying shades of brown, with Sylvia's being the lightest. All of them had freckles.

"Murder-Suicide Rocks Small New Hampshire Town"

An accurate headline, considering that even now, almost sixty years later, people didn't like talking about it. So many lives had been marred – Lester, Hannah's grandparents, Detective Engstrom (who I had no doubt was related to the missing Patricia Engstrom). Everyone who had been touched by the Dennis family had been devastated by Shirley's inexplicable actions.

The article added only one tidbit of information that I hadn't already known – that Sylvia, after being rescued from the hole and given medical attention, had gone to live with her father in New York.

"Sylvia Dennis New York," I muttered as I typed the words.

Apparently, there were quite a few Sylvia Dennises in New York, so I added "1960s" to my search. After a few more refinements of my key words, I came across a headline that made my stomach drop.

"Tragedy Continues for Dennis Family"

It was dated January of 1967, not even a year after the murder-suicide.

BROOKLYN, NY – Carl Dennis, 55, of Brooklyn died of a heart attack last Tuesday. Carl was the former husband of Shirley Dennis (née Flanagan), who was the perpetrator of a murder-suicide in small-town New Hampshire not quite one year ago. Shirley was also posthumously implicated in the disappearances of Kent Everett and Patricia Engstrom. The search continues...

I scanned to the bottom of the short article, looking for any mention of Sylvia, and finally I found it.

Carl's one remaining daughter has been sent to a children's home in New Hampshire.

"Why in God's name did they send her back to New Hampshire?" I wondered aloud.

Glancing up, I saw Monster lying at the bottom of the stairs, guilting me with his big brown eyes.

"Just a second," I told him as I typed in new search criteria – "New Hampshire children's homes".

Once again, there wasn't a ton of results, and when I added Sylvia's name to the search bar, the results were narrowed to zero. Instead, I went to each children's home website to see if they had archives or old pictures, but none of them did.

Thinking that maybe there had been different children's homes in the 60s, I tweaked my search and scanned photo after photo until I found what I wanted. There was Sylvia, now maybe 15 yet unmistakable with those freckles, standing in a group of other equally forlorn-looking kids. The photo's caption read: "Waterside Children's Home, 1972".

"Waterside... I think that's pretty close to here."

Sure enough, it was only twenty minutes away. I stared at the map on my screen, wondering whose brilliant idea it had been to send Sylvia to a home so close to the place where her mother and siblings had died brutal deaths. Wasn't she damaged enough?

Sighing and stretching, I looked down at Monster and realized that the light coming through the windows was deep orange. How could it be sunset already?

"Okay, I'm coming," I said, groaning as I stood. "Do you need another walk before dinner?"

Monster leapt to his feet and wagged his tail. I descended the stairs but paused as movement caught my eye. Through the glass storm door, I saw Lester emerge from the woods on the left, near the garage. He was shuffling along, muttering words I couldn't hear. Without a glance in my direction, he crossed over the driveway, sending bits of gravel skittering, and disappeared into the trees on the other side. As he walked, his right hand made that same strange waving motion:

Up, down, up, down. Left, right, left, right.

CHAPTER 10

THE NEXT TWO-AND-A-HALF WEEKS passed in a blur of hammers and nails, trips to Arden Woods, long walks, quick dinners, and restless sleep. Though I had filled my rented dumpster with debris from the downstairs bedroom and bathroom, it had quickly become apparent that I'd been too ambitious in my pre-Thanksgiving goals. The floors remained untouched, the glass wall cracked.

Two days before my trip to Indiana, time slowed to a grudging crawl. No point in starting on the floors or anything else when there wasn't enough time to make substantial progress, and I had no real reason to go into town since most places were closed for the holidays, so I spent a lot of time sitting around and checking the clock.

Knowing that my own excitement to see my family was the cause of time moving at a snail's pace, I tried not to think about them. However, on multiple occasions, I caught myself smiling as I imagined finally seeing Chloe in person again after three and a half months and teasing her about her nose ring. Texting just wasn't enough.

"Are you packed?" I asked her the day before we'd both be leaving.

"Ugh, no. You know I hate packing."

"I thought it was unpacking that you hated."

"Both."

"Didn't you leave your winter clothes at home?"

"Yeah. No need for parkas and long underwear here."

"Then just pack a toothbrush and wear the clothes you left in Indiana."

"Hm."

I moved the phone from my overheated right ear to my left. "What's up?"

"Oh, nothing."

"Chloe."

"No, it's fine."

"Tell me what's going on."

"Fine." She sighed. "I guess I'm just not sure this trip is a good idea."

"What? Why?"

"I don't know. I've barely gotten used to being here, and being away from everybody, and if I go back now..."

"If?" I held back a disbelieving scoff. "Didn't Mom and Dad already buy your plane ticket?"

"They could get a refund, right?"

"Chloe, come on. It's Thanksgiving. Aren't you excited?" She didn't answer, so I continued, hoping my voice held none of my anger or panic. "Mom's famous mashed potatoes. Dad's infamous cranberry jelly. Scrabble. Decorating for Christmas. It wouldn't be the same without you."

"Yeah, okay," Chloe said after a while, sounding marginally more cheerful. "I wouldn't want to miss Andy's annual rage over his favorite football team losing."

"Or Grandma's relentless questioning."

Chloe groaned. "I can hear it now." Putting on our grandma's low, southern-accented voice, she said, "'Los Angeles? It might mean City of Angels, but I can guarantee that it's the home of the devil.'"

"You think that's bad? Wait until she finds out about the divorce. 'Well, I suppose the popular stance these days is to accept such things. But you know what they say about how popular the path to hell is.'"

We both laughed, but it was an uneasy kind of laugh. I wished I hadn't brought up Grandma. I didn't want anything to discourage Chloe from coming.

"So, I'll see you in a few days?" I said.

"A few days," she echoed, which wasn't exactly an answer.

It took me a long time to fall asleep that night, and when I finally did, I dreamed about the house again. This time, I started inside the house, which was fixed and fully furnished. In the corner, Monster lounged on a large, squishy dog bed. Through the glass, I could see Hannah and Spencer on the back porch, laughing under strings of twinkling lights. I wanted to open the door and let them in, but I was in a hurry to leave. I put on one coat, then another, then another. Unable to lift my arm to turn the knob, I kicked the front door open.

As soon as I set foot outside, everything went dark and cold. Someone stood on the gravel between me and the garage. I knew it was Lester, even though his head was a rusty birdcage. When he spoke, sprays of feathers exploded from between the bars and stuck to my face, and I tried to go back inside, but the house had collapsed behind me.

I never should've left. I never should've left.

Twittering birds woke me, and I immediately jumped up. Based on the quantity and quality of sunlight, I had slept far later than I'd meant to.

"Get up, Monster, we've got to go!"

He was already stretching his long legs and yawning. Luckily, I had gotten everything ready the night before, even laying out the clothes I wanted to wear. All I needed to do was dress, brush my teeth, and load the truck.

When I opened the fridge to grab the sandwiches I'd made for the trip, I spotted a plastic dish of leftover chili in the back. Spur of the moment, I grabbed it.

So as not to encourage Lester's behavior of showing up unannounced through the woods, I drove the mile or so to his house and navigated the long, narrow, rutted driveway. Never having seen the front of his house, I was dismayed to find that it was nearly as run-down as my own.

If I ever finish my own house, maybe I could help with his.

Monster whined when I left him in the car. Though I knew he would never hurt a fly, I didn't want him to alarm Lester, especially since Lester had seemed more unhinged than usual lately.

"Hello?" I called, knocking on the front door. "It's Michelle. From down the road?"

A light flicked on inside. Moments later, Lester appeared, scratching his neck, which looked raw and red, like a freshly plucked chicken. His eyes were vague as they made their way up to my face. Holding out the container of chili, I forced a smile. Finally, he opened the door.

"I'm going out of town for a week or so," I said, resisting the urge to cough from my suddenly dry throat. "I have this leftover chili, and I wondered if you might want it."

He stared at the chili for an unbearably long time. Then, a reluctant smile cracked his face, and he took the container.

"Thanks, neighbor."

"I haven't seen you around much," I ventured. *And last time I did see you, you were waving your arms like a lunatic.* "Is everything okay?"

"Sure, sure."

"Look, I'm really sorry if what I said about... about my garage... upset you."

His eyes met mine, and they had sharpened. "Why don't you come in for a minute?"

"Um, well, I need to get on the road."

"Got a call from the police about your garage. Don't you want to know what they said?"

I had to admit; he was cleverer than I gave him credit for. For weeks, I had been dying to know what exactly – and *who* exactly – the police had found under the floor. They had gone through the garage one more time and asked me a few more questions but refused to answer any of mine.

"Okay," I said. "I've only got ten minutes, though."

Turning, he waved a hand over his shoulder to indicate that I should follow. I glanced at Monster, whose breath was fogging up the passenger window. He looked on the verge of barking, so I held a finger to my lips and mouthed: *Be right back.*

Every dingy, musty room we passed was heartbreakingly bare. The living room contained only a well-worn burgundy recliner, a metal TV tray, and a bulky wooden stand on which rested the oldest television I'd ever seen. The one bedroom I peeked into had a floor lamp with no bulb and a twin bed that looked like it hadn't been slept in for at least twenty years. A dusty quilt was folded neatly at its foot.

Even the walls were empty. Considering that Lester had lived here for decades, I had expected there to be photos. I didn't know if he had been married, but I knew – or at least strongly suspected – that he'd had a son. Then again, if his son really had disappeared, Lester probably didn't want to be constantly reminded of it.

The kitchen was as long and narrow as the driveway, with a tiny table crammed into the corner. Lester put the chili in the fridge, allowing me a glimpse of a jar of pickles, two bottles of beer, and nothing else. Then he sat at the table. I remained standing.

"How much do you already know?" he asked.

"Excuse me?"

"I'm sure you know all about it by now. If the police didn't tell you, that damn internet did."

No point in being coy. "You're talking about Shirley Dennis? And her kids?"

"And my kid," Lester grunted. "It wasn't him, by the way. It wasn't my Kent under your garage floor. It was the other one, the girl."

"Patricia Engstrom," I said, amazed that I could remember a name I'd only heard once but couldn't remember where I left my phone half the time. "Is she, I mean, *was* she related to Detective Engstrom?"

"Jimmy Engstrom. He wasn't even born when all this happened. After little Patty disappeared, her parents moved away and started over with a new house and new kids and everything. You know what they said about your garage?"

The question burst out of him, startling me.

"What?"

"They said it was brand new when the investigation started, foundation still wet, and they never even thought to look under there. Do you believe it? Some detectives. That woman poured the cement herself to hide all those bones when she heard the police were sniffing around."

"That seems like pretty meticulous planning. I thought she was kind of, you know, crazy. You'd have to be to do what she did."

Lester was silent for a minute, scraping one thick, yellow fingernail over a hole in the tablecloth. The tablecloth seemed out of place, given the sparseness of the rest of the house. Maybe it was a leftover ritual from when he'd had a family. In spite of how sorry I felt for him, my mind was on my own family, and I had to resist checking my watch.

"That's the weird thing," said Lester in a low voice, almost as if he were talking to himself. "She wasn't crazy, at least not in the beginning. She and Madeline were fast friends. The kids all played together in the woods. We had them over for pizza every single Friday."

I thought about my first night in the house – a Friday night – when I'd seen Lester alone in his yard with boxes of pizza. No family. No friends. My nose stung with unexpected emotion.

"And then," Lester continued, "she got that damn bird."

"The eared nightjar?"

"They named it Simon, after Shirley's oldest boy. They were so proud the day they got him, showing him off. We all knew it was illegal, but that didn't matter around here. Kent was smitten. Said the thing looked like a dragon from Lord of the Rings."

Lester let out a sad chuckle.

I could picture the scene perfectly – Simon the dragon-bird in his golden cage, disoriented by the unfamiliar surroundings and the excited screeches of four young children; Lester and Madeline, who I assumed was his wife, watching from a distance with their arms around each other. Shirley staring at the bird and thinking...what? How could a mother with big plans for her future snap like that?

"That was a good day," Lester said, his smile fading. "The last good day for a long time."

"What happened?"

He rubbed the bridge of his nose and sighed. Despite my desire to hit the road, I was completely drawn in. Ever since Hannah told me about the murders, I hadn't been able to get them out of my head.

"One night, just about a month after they got the bird, I heard her screaming all the way from here. Ran out the door in my pajama bottoms, grabbed my shotgun. Thought a bear got in the house or something. When I got there, she was dragging her boy, Simon, outside by the hair. Tossed him on the ground. He was twelve at the time, but skinny as a reed. I shouted for her to stop, and then I saw she had a knife."

"Jesus," I said as a chill ran from my scalp to my toes.

"Quick as I could, I held her back. She kept saying, 'That's not my Simon! That's not him! It's a monster!' Madeline was there at that point. I told her to go inside and call the police. They took Shirley away for the night to calm down, and the kids spent the night at our house."

"I bet they were freaked out."

"The little girls not so much. Don't think they really knew what was happening. At about 3 AM, I caught the boy sneaking out. He told me he needed to feed the bird. Refused to go to bed until he did. So I took him back to the house and went up with him. The bird was kept in an upstairs bedroom. Boy had to undo three or four locks to get in."

"Those locks are still there," I said. "Why on earth did she do that?"

"I asked the boy that same question. He looked real uneasy. Told me his ma thought the bird was a demon and said it was talking inside her head."

I swallowed uncomfortably. "What did the bird say?"

"Don't know," said Lester with a sniff. "But it must've been real convincing."

"You think it told her to kill her kids?"

"No telling." He leaned forward, resting his elbows on the table. "But when I picked Shirley up the next day from the police station and brought her home, she didn't want to take the kids back. Said they weren't hers."

I recalled what Hannah had said about the suicide note, and there was part of me that really wanted to read it, hoping it could make sense of what happened back then and what was happening to me now.

"Madeline talked to her," Lester continued. "Convinced her that she needed to care for her children."

Probably not the best idea, given what happened.

"Next week, Kent came back from that house all shook up. Wouldn't tell me what happened, but he wasn't the same after that, and he kept..." Lester trailed off, making the up, down, left, right motion with his hand. "Doctor said it was a nervous tic, nothing to worry about. Lord knows what he saw in that house. Four weeks later, he went missing, and a year after that, Madeline was gone too."

The lump in my throat made it difficult to breathe. I didn't need to ask what had happened to Madeline. Whether she had died of grief or run from it, I could see the end result sitting in front of me, old and weary and alone, his grief so palpable that the air around us felt heavy.

"What do you think Simon – the bird, that is – had to do with all this?" I asked. "You said things started to go downhill once Shirley brought the bird home, but why?"

Lester pushed himself up, joints creaking, and left the room. I feared I'd pried too far, but then he returned, carrying a large photograph. He handed it to me, and I smoothed it out on the table. The creases were not the random ones of a piece of trash, but the well-worn creases of a page often looked at.

"Buddy on the force gave me this," said Lester, sitting again. "Used to read it all the time. Thought it might'a had a clue about Kent."

Something told me that Lester *still* frequently read the note from the crime scene photograph before me. In the photo, the note, which was scrawled and blotted on a sheet of stationery, was lit up so brightly that the words were almost bleached out. It had obviously been taken at night with a bright flash, probably moments after they'd found Shirley's body.

He took my children away somewhere, and I keep waiting, but they haven't come home yet. If you find them in the hole, that's not really them, they're imposters. I don't know who they are. I don't recognize them. I put them down there so they'd tell me where the real children are, but they're not talking. They're so quiet now. Just like Patty and Kent, so quiet, not talking. Don't let them out. Don't let him out. That damned bird. I'm getting him out of my head. If the children come home, tell them I did it to save them. Tell them mother loves them.

"Oh my god," I said once I'd read the note twice. "Shirley thought the bird replaced her kids with imposters, and that's why she threw them in the hole. That's why she killed them."

But how could a mother not recognize her own children, the people she saw every day and loved and cherished? Well, I knew the answer to that – dementia.

"Actually," Lester began, but I cut him off.

"I have to go," I said, standing abruptly. "Thank you for telling me all that."

"And thank you for the chili."

Lester walked me to the door and gave a half-hearted wave. I was so distracted as I turned onto the road that I nearly hit a Land Rover. Its long, irate honk barely registered.

That's not really them...they're imposters.

Dementia. Alcohol-induced dementia. That might not have been what Shirley had, but it was what the doctor had told me I had...and it was getting worse.

Chapter 11

Driving through the town I'd spent the first thirty-three-and-a-half years of my life in was a surreal experience, the strangeness heightened by the fact that I arrived in the middle of the night, having ignored my mom's suggestion to stop in Cincinnati. I wouldn't have been able to sleep, anyway. Since my conversation with Lester, my brain hadn't shut up for a single second.

Muscle memory alone prompted me to take the right exit and every subsequent turn along mostly empty streets. My actual memory was surprisingly lacking. Buildings and houses jutted up out of nowhere, none of them familiar.

Confusion.

Suggestibility.

Irritability.

Those were only a few of the symptoms the doctor had mentioned.

"Over time," she'd said, *"you may begin to lose even simple memories, such as where you went to school, who your friends were, or where you grew up."*

"I'm just tired," I burst out, making Monster lift his head. "I've been driving for sixteen hours."

But when I turned onto Walnut Court, where my parents lived, it wasn't the correct street; the street I'd grown up on, the street I'd learned to drive on, the street Andy and I had chased each other down on roller blades. It wasn't wide enough. The houses were completely different. And had that big tree always been there? I searched my mind unsuccessfully for a childhood memory of it.

Then I saw my parents' house, and everything fell into its correct and comfortable place. Pulling up to the curb, I put the truck in park, rested my head against the steering wheel, and took a few deep breaths.

It's okay to forget things when you make new memories. Besides, you haven't actually lived here in years.

This wasn't strictly true. After the separation, I had briefly moved back in, but did that really count? A small voice in the back of my head reminded me that even when I'd lived with Daniel, we had come over here once a week for dinner.

"Shut up," I told the voice. "I'm fine."

The house was a much more modern design than any I'd seen in New Hampshire. Navy shutters stood out against gray bricks. Warm light shone through the curtained living room window; it was the same lamp my mom left on every night. White and yellow pansies filled the flower beds; my parents planted them together each winter.

So he wouldn't trample the flowers, I kept Monster on his leash. He had lived here too, for a while. My parents loved dogs, though they hadn't had one in years; unlike Daniel, they had welcomed Monster with open arms. His favorite napping spot had been on the couch with my dad, and my mom had bought a white ceramic jar just for his treats. She had probably filled it up for this week.

"Shh," I said to Monster as I fumbled with my keys. "Don't wake up Grandma and Grandpa."

As expected, there was nobody downstairs, and the house had been closed up for the night. Now that I was inside, things seemed more familiar. My eyes automatically traveled to the large, framed family photo over the fireplace. It was a few years old, meaning that Daniel was in it, and my nieces and nephew were noticeably younger.

"I know what I'm getting Mom for Christmas," I muttered.

We made our way upstairs as quietly as possible. Countless other photos lined the wall – me at age fourteen with braces and awful chunky highlights; Andy in his high school soccer uniform; Andy and Christy's wedding portrait; Chloe as a baby, wearing nothing but a diaper and sunglasses; all three of us kids, sunburnt and freckly, standing by the neighborhood pool.

"Chloe?" I called softly when I reached the upper landing.

No light peeked under her door. She had to be here, though; her flight was supposed to arrive long before I did. In my rush this morning, I hadn't checked in with her. Come to think of it, it was odd that she hadn't texted to say she'd made it home.

"Chloe?"

Without knocking, I pushed her door open. The room was cold and obviously unlived-in. Pulling free of my grip, Monster did a lap around the room, nose to the floor. Then he sat at the foot of the bed and whined.

"I don't know where she is, buddy."

We crossed the hall to the guest room that had once, many years ago, been my room and had become my room again briefly over the summer. I set my bag down and unclipped Monster's leash so he could investigate while I checked my phone, which didn't have a single message. I even tried turning it off and on again, but still nothing.

Not caring what time it was on the West coast, I called Chloe.

"Where are you?" I asked before she could even say hello. "Did your flight get delayed?"

"Didn't Mom and Dad tell you?"

"No, they're asleep. I just got here."

"I can't make it," Chloe said. "I've got too much going on."

Each word was a punch in my gut. The sensible part of my brain shut down, leaving nothing but rage and deep, bitter sadness.

"Too much going on?" I repeated. "Are you *so* busy getting just the right shot for Instagram?"

"It's harder than it looks."

The joke did not make me smile. "Yeah, it must be time-consuming doing...I'm sorry, what exactly are you doing? Commercial work obviously doesn't involve much."

"Actually, I got a real job," she said stiffly.

"Let me guess – the lead in a Netflix series? No, wait – were you hand-selected to star in the next Marvel movie?"

There was a long pause. "It's at a coffee shop."

"Oh, well, now that I know it's a job that couldn't wait until after Thanksgiving."

"Why are you being like this?"

She didn't sound angry, just hurt. I was hurting her. But I couldn't stop.

"Because I don't understand why you would bail on me at the last second."

"I'm not bailing on you."

"You said you'd be here, and you're not."

"I...I just want to get used to being in LA. I want to adjust, and I can't do that if I'm always going back to the last place I lived."

"You mean *home*?"

"LA is my home now. And New Hampshire is yours."

"That's bullshit. You may not think of this as home anymore, but it's where most of your family is," I said, trying to hide the tremble in my voice. "Don't you want to see us? Are you seriously never coming back?"

"Of course I'll come back, maybe every Christmas."

"So, what? I'll only see you once a year for the rest of my life?"

"Don't say it like that."

For the first time, I noticed that her voice was tremulous, too. I tried to see it from her point of view, being only 23 and suddenly out alone in the world, thousands of miles away from the people who loved you. It couldn't have been easy. I was being an immature brat, and I knew it, but I wanted her to hurt as much as I was hurting.

"Have fun being alone on Thanksgiving," I said, then hung up and turned off my phone.

For the next five hours, I lay in my old bed under its new, stiff bedspread, staring up at the same crack in the ceiling that had always been there, replaying everything I'd said to Chloe. I was being unfair, *ridiculously* unfair and insane. I was thirty-fucking-three, and my own baby sister was acting more mature and well-adjusted than me.

When had I become so clingy with her? Chloe had been only eight when I'd left for college, and I'd moved in with Daniel right after. Our life stages couldn't have been more different. In fact, after I got married and took on more responsibilities at work, I hardly saw Chloe for a few years. We texted sometimes, but our lives were so separate.

This past summer, that had changed. We were living in the same house again for the first time in fifteen years, and we realized just how much we had in common. We watched old black-and-white movies, inserting our own dialogue into the silent ones. We went hiking every weekend; I taught her how to build a fire, and she taught me how to French braid my hair. We talked about anything and everything.

Finally, one clear and starry night, she had confided in me, saying: "I always thought Daniel was way too boring for you."

"You did?"

"Yeah, like, last year on your birthday, he gave you diamond earrings?" She snorted.

"What's wrong with that? Diamond earrings are a great gift."

"They're so generic. Like what a guy buys when he has no idea what you actually like. Same thing applies to lotion and candles."

"He got me lotion and candles every Valentine's Day," I admitted. "I had a secret stash at the back of the linen closet because they weren't even the scents I like."

"See? Exactly! You are not generic, and you deserve better than generic gifts from a generic husband."

Somehow, she had taken every frustration that had been building up inside me for years and summed them up in one sentence. While the rest of my family had acted disapproving and confused about the divorce, Chloe had supported it one hundred percent, acting like it was about time she got her real sister back. Even I had had my doubts, but in that moment, I realized that if Chloe had been married to someone like Daniel, I would've told her to ditch him, and that made me secure in my decision.

That summer, she had been there when I needed her most. And now, she was gone.

My finger traced a pattern on the cold, white sheet – up, down, left, right, up, down, left, right. I couldn't seem to stop. I knew the motion came from somewhere, but I couldn't place it. After a while, my fingertip became raw from the repetition.

Inch by inch, the sun crept through my window. Car doors slammed, and ice-cold engines cranked. Downstairs, my parents conversed in low voices, and the coffeemaker beeped. A few minutes later, the doorbell rang. Monster's head jerked up, and his breathing quickened. Rapid footsteps crossed the threshold, accompanied by high-pitched voices. Monster whined.

"All right, all right," I groaned. "Give me a second."

⚬

"Misha, Misha!"

My youngest niece, Karly, threw herself at me the moment I set foot in the living room.

"It's Michelle," corrected 13-year-old Ava, putting her hands on her narrow hips. "Stop talking like a baby."

Karly stuck out her tongue at her sister and then turned her attention to Monster, giggling shrilly as he licked her face. My nephew, Aiden, was on the couch, hidden behind whatever new handheld gaming system he'd gotten recently; he didn't so much as acknowledge my presence.

"Hello, Michelle," said Ava loftily, holding out her hand as if we were adults greeting each other at a dinner party.

"Hello," I said, shaking her hand.

A pang went through me as I imagined the look Chloe and I would've shared at this parody of adulthood. She would've made a mock bow and said, in a high-brow accent, *"Good day, old chap. Fancy meeting you. How in blazes are you?"* Then, after Ava undoubtedly marched away in annoyance, Chloe would've rolled her eyes and smirked.

"Hey," I said, leaning in so the others wouldn't hear me. "I brought you a present."

"You did?" In spite of her attempts to appear grown-up, I could tell she was excited. "What is it?"

"It's a surprise. And a secret, because I didn't get anything for Karly or Aiden."

"Okay," she said, nodding solemnly.

Just then, my mom bustled into the room. Though it was a little chilly in the house, she was wearing her usual strappy sandals with jeans and a white linen blouse. Bright red toes indicated a recent pedicure. Her whole familiar ensemble and demeanor, and her hair that was the exact same color as Chloe's, inexplicably made me want to cry.

"All right, pancakes are ready," she said, clapping her hands. "Butter and syrup on the counter."

Aiden hopped off the couch and raced Karly into the kitchen. Ava followed at a more dignified pace, as if determined to show that she was more mature than her siblings. Once they were gone, my mom pulled me into a bone-crushing hug, enveloping me in the scent of maple syrup.

"Hey, sweetie," she said, rubbing my back and scratching it gently with her long nails. "You must've gotten in late last night."

"A little after two."

"Goodness! Sorry for all the commotion so early. I'm sure you could've used more sleep."

"What are they doing here, anyway? Don't they have school?"

"They got the whole week off, lucky ducks."

"Lucky," I agreed, avoiding my mom's gaze, wondering if Chloe had called her yet. "But if the school is closed, why can't Andy watch them?"

The kids went to a private school that also had a high school, at which Andy was the girls' soccer coach. Chloe and I often joked (only somewhat bitterly) that our parents probably wished we were more like Andy – All-American soccer coach; beautiful wife who's a hard-working nurse and excellent baker; three smart kids; big house in the suburbs; content to remain in the same town for the rest of his life.

"Oh, he's got some teacher development training today and tomorrow," my mom said.

"Wow, even the coaches have to do sh- stuff like that?"

Mom frowned slightly. "He's been teaching geography, too, for about two years now. Remember?"

"Right," I said quickly. "It's just hard to picture him as a teacher. He's much more at home on the soccer field."

"That's true enough."

Surely by now Chloe had called to tell her and Dad what happened last night, to tell them that I'd lost my mind. But my mom either didn't know or didn't want to discuss it yet.

Unable to stand the neglect anymore, Monster pawed at my mom's leg and whined.

"I haven't forgotten you," she assured him, petting his head. "I've got a nice juicy ham bone in the fridge with your name on it. Dad fixed up those holes in the backyard, so do you mind keeping an eye on him whenever he goes out so he doesn't tear the grass up?"

"Sure," I said. "He's much better about that now."

"Moving out of that puppy phase?"

"Finally."

Angry shouts from the kitchen – Aiden had taken the last piece of bacon from Ava, whose mature façade had crumbled. As I listened to my mom's attempts to make peace, the scene looked more like a movie than real life. I felt removed from it, a viewer rather than a participant. I had the sudden, strange sensation that I was still in New Hampshire, watching my family through a screen. Only they weren't really my family, they were actors; similar but not exactly the same. Imposters.

Chapter 12

THAT SENSATION OF DISCONNECTION faded over the next few days, though I still got flashes of it from time to time. I would wake up in the middle of the night with no idea where I was. My mom would mention a person I was supposed to know, and probably had known, and I would have no idea who she was talking about. During a game of Scrabble, I would look across the table and wonder who that gray-haired man was, only to remember it was my dad.

Every time it happened, I attributed it to tiredness or hunger or distraction, though in the back of my mind, I began to think something was seriously wrong.

"You okay?" my dad asked me on Wednesday.

I looked up, not sure when I had settled on the couch in the living room. A football game was on, which usually meant I'd rather be anywhere else. How long had I been sitting there?

"Fine," I said. "Just tired."

"I'm not surprised. I hear you walking around at two in the morning."

This was news to me.

"That might be Monster," I said, trying to brush it off. "He gets restless."

My dad cleared his throat twice, a sure sign that he was about to bring up an uncomfortable topic. "It wasn't Monster standing in the backyard last night."

Too shocked to cover for myself, I blurted, "I was in the backyard last night?"

"Got up to get a glass of water and noticed the back door was open. Nearly had a heart attack when I saw you out there."

"What... um, what was I doing?"

"Staring up into the sugar maple. I tried to talk to you, but you didn't answer, just kept crossing yourself like a Catholic in church. Finally got you to come inside with me."

"I don't remember that at all," I admitted, then added jokingly, "But don't worry, I haven't converted to Catholicism."

"Misha..."

"It's not that, Daddy, I swear."

"Have you been doing okay up there? Going to your meetings?"

"I don't want to talk about it."

Aiden entered the room, saw what was on TV, and immediately asked a question about a certain player, giving me an opening to leave. My mom and Karly were out getting the inevitable last-minute groceries for tomorrow's meal. Ava sat at the kitchen table, watching video tutorials on fancy napkin-folding. With a fresh cup of coffee, I sat down in the chair next to hers.

"Are you in charge of place settings?" I asked.

"I guess," she said vaguely, focused on the video.

"Remember last year, when Aunt Chloe made those cute pine cone centerpieces?"

"I helped," she said indignantly. "Like, a lot."

"Maybe you and I could come up with something cool like that and make it today."

At last, Ava set the phone aside and gave me her full attention. Her thin lips twisted to one side, and her dark eyebrows lowered. "You've been so weird."

The comment caught me off-guard. "I have? How?"

"Like, just now, you said we should make a centerpiece, and I asked what kind, and you didn't answer. You sat there and stared into space for like five minutes."

"I guess I didn't hear you."

"You do it all the time now, like you're somewhere far away. Everyone thinks it's weird. And what's up with the hand thing?"

She pointed at my hand, which I noticed was tracing the up, down, left, right pattern on the table. I put my hand in my lap. If I had been doing that a lot, no wonder my family thought I was losing my mind. It was this place. It didn't feel like home anymore, didn't feel like I belonged in it. I was not myself here.

Ava was still looking at me, and I wondered if I'd zoned out again.

"I'm fine," I said. "Let's get ideas for the centerpieces."

"Fine. And by the way, you still haven't given me my present."

What present? I wondered as Ava typed "Thanksgiving centerpieces" into her phone. The results appeared right as the doorbell rang.

"I'll get it," I said. "You keep looking."

My legs shook as I left the kitchen, and I was too warm. The heating in this house was always up too high. I tugged off my sweatshirt and draped it over the stair railing, then opened the front door.

The man on the porch had thinning brown hair, a messy goatee, and a pronounced Adam's apple. He was wearing a rumpled blue long-sleeved polo shirt, and his eyes were bloodshot, and he was looking at me like I was a lighthouse on a dark sea. I was about to ask who he was when it hit me.

"Daniel? How did you know I was here?" I demanded.

His gaze remained locked on mine. "I ran into Andy at the gas station yesterday."

Thanks a lot, Andy.

"Well, what are you doing here?" I asked, crossing my arms over my chest.

"You really don't know?"

"Not even a little bit."

"Michelle."

He said my name with such familiarity and such sadness, but what did he have to be sad about? His life was ultimately better without me, just as mine was better without him.

"I really don't know," I reiterated with an exaggerated shrug.

He turned slightly away, and I noticed again how wrinkled his shirt was. It had most likely stayed balled up in the laundry basket for weeks before he hung it up. A light breeze blew, and I caught a whiff of his cologne, which he very rarely wore. Realizing that he'd put it on for me, my heart softened a little.

"How are you doing?" I asked, and I truly wanted to know.

"Better," he said after a moment. "Had a rough couple of months."

He looked like he wanted to say more, like he was weighing his words carefully. He had always been good – too good – at hiding his emotions. Just like he'd been too good at ignoring mine.

"Hang on a second," he said.

He popped the trunk of his obnoxiously red car, which was parked at the curb, and heaved out a large cardboard box. When he set it down gently on the porch, I peeked inside.

"Monster's bed," I said, pointing at it. "And my CDs. Thanks."

"You would've had them weeks ago if you'd just given me your address like you said you would."

I frowned. "I said that?"

"Are you kidding?" He seemed more frustrated than angry. "After you... when you left, you said you didn't have room to take everything, and that when you found a place to live, you'd give me your new address so I could ship a few boxes to you."

"Okay." I had no memory of that.

"I didn't hear from you, so I tried calling, but you changed your number?"

"It seemed like the right thing to do."

"Why are you acting like I'm some psycho stalker? I thought everything between us was amicable. Are you..." He swallowed hard. "Are you still drinking?"

"No," I spat. "Are you?"

"No." He reached into his pocket and pulled out a coin. "Thirty days sober, actually."

I stared at the coin, anger rising inside me like some out of control water leak.

"Great," I said, voice dripping with sarcasm. "Thirty days. Bravo."

"It's actually a good start," he mumbled.

"Hm. Or maybe a good start would've been not drinking at all and not dragging me into it."

"I didn't—"

"Or maybe you should've fucking listened to me when I said we had a problem, but now it's too late, and Simon..." I covered my mouth with my hand.

"What are you talking about? Who is Simon?"

"Is everything okay?" My dad had appeared, looking concerned, eyes moving from me to Daniel and back again.

"This is ridiculous," Daniel said. "I only brought over a few things that she left at our house because she never gave me her new address like she said she would."

"I never said that," I insisted.

"Why don't you go on inside, Michelle," my dad said, putting a warm hand on my shoulder. "I'll talk to Daniel for a minute."

Before the door closed, I caught a glimpse of Daniel's confused expression. Quickly, I moved into the living room and peeked between the blinds. I didn't have a full view of the front porch, so all I could see was the back of my dad's head and half of Daniel's face. Whatever my dad was saying made Daniel deeply uncomfortable and...sad? A few minutes later, he nodded and left, jamming his hands into his pockets. I stepped away from the window right as my dad came back inside, carrying the box.

"What did you tell him?" I asked, surprised at the accusatory tone of my own voice.

"That you're having a hard time right now, and he needs to take it easy."

"Having a hard time? I'm not having a hard time. I'm better than ever."

His warm, calm, social-worker gaze remained on me, and I couldn't meet it. Once again, I wondered if he'd heard from Chloe, if they'd all been talking about me behind my back and deciding I was crazy.

"I guess I am pretty tired," I said slowly. "And I have a headache now."

Sighing, he put the box down and approached me. "It's more than that, Misha. You're forgetting things."

"I don't have a great memory. So what?"

"Come here."

Sitting on the stiff, formal sofa that nobody used, he patted the firm cushion next to him. I sat, hugging my knees to my chest and feeling like a child about to be scolded, yet my dad looked more sad than angry. He looked old, too, like he'd aged ten years in the last few months.

He cleared his throat once, twice, thrice.

"Before you left for New Hampshire, Daniel came by and brought you some things. Your tool box, a suitcase. I heard you tell him you didn't have room for it all, and that you'd give him your address once you got settled so he could ship the remainder to you."

"I did?"

"You even said you'd pay the shipping costs. You two were on good terms. Now you're treating him like a dangerous ex from some true crime documentary."

"He *is* my ex now, daddy."

"Yes, but he's still Daniel. Even though it didn't work out between you, he's still the guy who made us all watch Sharknado, the guy who helped put up our Christmas lights every year. He's not a weirdo; he's Daniel."

"You're right," I said as guilt crept in. "I shouldn't have been so rude to him. I feel stupid now."

"You're not stupid. You're sick."

"I'm not sick."

"A lot of the children I work with, their own parents don't recognize them anymore because of—"

"I don't want to talk about this."

He nodded slowly. "Well, you need to talk to someone, even if it's not me."

The door to the garage flew open, and my mom and Karly entered, arms laden with paper grocery bags. Right behind them came Andy and Christy, hauling a real Christmas tree. My dad jumped up to help, and I took the opportunity to slip upstairs unnoticed. It was at least ten degrees colder up there, so I switched to thicker socks and put my sweatshirt back on. Then I sat on the edge of the bed that had once been mine, though now it had a new covering.

From downstairs, the voices of my family jumbled together into one constant rumble, occasionally peppered with laughter. A year ago, I would've been down there with them, completely content. Instead, I felt like a bird snatched from its faraway home and forced into a cage in a stranger's house.

———————⋅◦⋅———————

WHEN I AWOKE ON Thanksgiving Day, my arms were unbearably itchy. Half-asleep, I rolled onto my back and scratched them frantically from shoulder to elbow, over and over. It was comforting and satisfying, and then, without warning, excruciating.

Jolting upright, I opened my eyes. Bloody gashes streaked my upper arms. Skin and viscera caked beneath my fingernails. Raw flesh burned in the open air, yet still I longed to scratch.

I stumbled into the hall bathroom and fumbled in the drawers for bandages and disinfectant. As I washed my arms with soap and warm water, as I gritted my teeth against the sting of iodine, as I clumsily applied bandages to the worst spots, I had to fight the all-consuming urge to keep scratching.

There was a tap on the bathroom door and my dad said, "Misha? Are you okay?"

"Fine," I said.

A quick glance in the mirror told me that opening the door would do nothing to reassure him. Even aside from my torn-up arms, I looked awful. My cheeks were gaunt. Clumps of hair were missing from my scalp. In horrified fascination, I touched the bare spots as tears pricked my eyes.

"Want me to bring you a cup of coffee?"

"That's okay, I'm about to take a shower. Be down in half an hour."

I turned the water on and listened at the door until he was gone. Then I darted back across the hall, grabbed clean clothes, and retreated to the bathroom once more. Afraid that a full shower would be too painful, I washed my hair in the tub and dabbed at the rest of my body with a wet cloth. Patches of dry skin sent that urge to scratch screaming through me. I found a half-empty bottle of lotion and slathered it over my entire body. The blow-dryer did my thin, patchy hair little good. How could it be this bad when yesterday it had been its normal, thick, wavy self? There was no way it would go unnoticed.

I dressed warmly, using a soft gray beanie from one of Chloe's drawers to hide my abysmal hair. If anyone questioned it, I'd just say I was cold. They couldn't find that suspicious when it felt like an Arctic tundra in the house.

Chloe's old room still smelled like her – peppermint and hairspray. Unlike my room, hers hadn't been empty long enough to convert into a craft room or home gym. It was exactly the way she'd left it, minus the items she'd taken to LA. I lingered for a moment, running a finger over the spines of the old school textbooks she'd refused to throw away or sell. *"What if I need to look something up?"* she'd said, ignoring me when I reminded her of that thing called the internet. She could be strangely old-fashioned like that at times.

I hadn't spoken to or texted Chloe since our fight. Honestly, I wasn't sure *how* to talk to her after that. She had said it was easier to stay put for a while in order to adjust, but what she meant was that it was easier not to see me or the rest of our family. Seeing the people you loved made it that much harder to leave them again.

Maybe she's right. It's better to forget.

My parents gave only the slightest indication that they thought my hat was an odd choice, but they let it slide.

"Do I need to go pick up Grandma?" I asked as I poured a cup of coffee.

"Oh, she can't make it this year," Dad said with a sigh. "Actually, she said she'd rather have the nursing home Thanksgiving dinner."

My mom mouthed *"small mercies"*, and I grinned.

I added cream and sugar to my coffee, asked my dad about his work, and helped my mom peel potatoes. Normal. So normal. Andy, Christy, and the kids arrived around nine, and we all sat around the table to eat breakfast casserole. It had never been my favorite, but it was at least warm. Still, it didn't touch the coldness that gripped my very core.

Afterward, I ducked upstairs to add another layer of socks, and Andy, Aiden, and Karly went to the front yard to toss a football around. There was a lot of prep work to be done, so I returned to the kitchen, pausing outside when I heard low, tense voices.

"—mentioned it, too," my mom said. "She's worried."

"I'm worried too," said Christy. "She looks like she hasn't slept in a month, and she only ate two bites at breakfast. Do you think she'd let me take a look?"

"It wouldn't hurt to try," said my dad. "Though I don't think the problem is entirely physical."

"Are they talking about you again?"

I jumped, hitting my head against a metal wall sconce. White spots bloomed in my vision, and I blinked rapidly. Ava had come up behind me, wearing a paper chef's hat and holding the leather-bound, hand-written family cookbook that had been passed down for generations.

"What do you mean, 'again'?" I whispered, rubbing the top of my head.

"They've been doing it a lot, like whenever you leave the room. I told you – they think you're acting weird. And why are you wearing a hat?"

"It's cold."

"No, it isn't."

"Well, why are *you* wearing a hat?" I retorted.

"It's a *chef's* hat." She rolled her eyes – a gesture at which she excelled. "Because we're *cooking*."

Chin raised, she marched into the kitchen, and I followed, giving my family enough time to position themselves like they'd been doing anything but having a secret conversation about me. My dad was rinsing a colander full of cranberries, my mom was julienning carrots, and Christy was arranging a festive tablecloth.

Ava raised an eyebrow at me, snatched up a stack of cloth napkins, and started folding.

"What can I do to help?" I asked.

Our kitchen always got hectic on Thanksgiving – too many people cooking too many things at once. Mostly, I stayed on the fringes, waiting until asked to peel another two potatoes or get the pie crust out of the freezer in the garage. Around two, when the craziness was at its peak, I took Monster into the backyard and let him run around, chasing the kids (except Ava, who was far too dignified for that). I couldn't help glancing repeatedly at the sugar maple, expecting to see Simon the eared nightjar's shape in the branches.

"Aunt Misha!"

"Huh?"

Snapping out of a daze, I looked down to find Karly standing there, wide-eyed and pale.

"What's wrong, Kar?"

Mutely, she pointed at my left arm. Blood had seeped through the many layers of bandages, shirts, and sweaters, making my sleeve look like it had been painted red, dripping from the cuff, hitting the back patio with a soft *plip, plip, plip*.

"It's okay," I said quickly. "I just got a cut when I was working on my new house, and I guess it opened up again."

"It's so much," she said, her voice monotone with shock. "It's a lot of blood."

"It's fine, I promise. You keep playing with Monster, and I'll go clean up."

Thanksgiving dinner was loud and frantic, with arms reaching for various dishes and random bits of laughter coming out of nowhere. The others were pink-cheeked, but I huddled inside my layers, trying not to let my teeth chatter when I spoke. My fingernails were periwinkle at the cuticles.

The thought of Chloe alone in her apartment eating a sad frozen meal or Chinese takeout made me ache. Relenting, I picked up my phone to text her and saw a notification for a new Instagram post. Chloe didn't look sad or lonely. Chloe was wearing a plaid apron and posing with one of her roommates – Lola? Lyla? – as she stirred a dish of macaroni and cheese.

@chloster99: Friendsgiving in LA! Missing home, though <3

So, she wished she was here after all. My heart thawed. If only the rest of my body would do the same.

ORIGINALLY, I HADN'T PLANNED to leave until the next Monday, but after another night's terrible sleep and the threat of being poked and prodded by Christy, I wanted more than ever to get back to New Hampshire. I was tired of spending so much energy trying to convince people that I was okay.

When I brought my suitcase down and set it by the front door, my dad emerged from the kitchen holding a mug of coffee. For a moment, I saw him as if from the outside, like I was a stranger standing in his home, a place I didn't belong.

"Where you going?" he asked, puzzled but smiling.

"New Hampshire. Thought I'd head home early."

"I thought Ava was coming over today to help you with something."

I searched my memory but found nothing about this. A wall had formed in my brain, and I had no idea how much it was blocking out.

"It's kind of an emergency," I said, unlocking the door and letting Monster out. "My neighbor called and said that a pipe burst. He's taking care of it for now, but I really need to get back."

Whether he bought the lie or not, I couldn't tell. I told him and my mom goodbye, promised to text when I made it safely, and evaded questions about if I'd be home for Christmas. Monster and I piled into the truck, and we were gone. Only when we made it to the interstate did I realize I'd left the box from Daniel and my coat behind.

CHAPTER 13

COMING BACK TO NEW Hampshire was nothing like coming back to Indiana. Everything from the tilt of the trees to the fresh smell of the air was familiar. I told myself it was a good sign. I was finally learning to view this place as home.

Snow had fallen while we were gone, and the sides of the roads were piled high with icy, gray-white lumps.

"I hope it snows again soon, buddy," I said to Monster, whose head was hanging out the open passenger window. "I know you saw a lot of snow in Indiana, but this will be next level."

As we traveled down the road that my driveway branched off from, I suddenly felt like I was in one of my dreams. There were no other cars. Even with the windows down, it was eerily silent. I blinked hard a few times and pinched my arm, forgetting about the still-raw scratches. I hissed in a breath and gritted my teeth.

Yep. Definitely awake.

Over the river. Past the large rock that indicated Lester's driveway. Midnight was not far off. Slowing down in case of ice, I turned into my driveway. The instant the house came into view, in spite of the darkness, I knew something was wrong. Once more, I had the overpowering sensation of being in a dream.

"Stay here," I told Monster, leaving him in the truck with the windows up.

The front door wouldn't budge. Hurrying around to the back, I leapt up the steps to the deck, turned on my phone flashlight, and stared in horror through the glass wall. My knees hit the hard, frosty wood. In a way, it *was* like my dreams – in them, I had been sure that without me there, the entire house would crumble to pieces.

The loft had collapsed. Beams and plaster and wires littered the living room. Some of them had landed on the new kitchen counters, which I could tell from here were cracked and filthy. Almost everything I had worked so hard on for months was ruined.

I would have to start over.

When I got inside and began picking through the wreckage, it became clear what had triggered the collapse – I had forgotten to install a new spiral staircase. It wasn't the only support for the loft, of course, but I had noticed the floor sagging where the spiral staircase used to be, and that weight must have caused the other supports to snap.

Day one, I distinctly remembered making a note about the staircase. Every single day since I'd moved in, I had passed by the studs in the floor where the staircase would be attached, so why hadn't I installed it yet?

Making my way carefully, I saw that a beam had somehow wedged against the front door, preventing it from opening. When I heaved it aside, I saw a long scratch in the wood that I'd painted gray not two weeks ago, the gray that Chloe had suggested.

In that moment, I wanted nothing more than to curl up into a ball and sleep for 12 hours. With a sigh, I climbed the stairs, thankful that they hadn't been structurally damaged any more than they already were. The bedrooms were also miraculously untouched. But the secret, sound-proofed room was completely destroyed. The cages, the mattress – all of it had fallen through into the living room. The only thing that remained was the poem carved into the ceiling and...something shiny?

Underneath the poem, a silver necklace had been nailed to the wood. Its dangling amethyst pendant rotated gently counterclockwise. A memory prickled at the back of my mind, then it slipped away like drops of water on a windshield.

"Hello? Michelle, are you in there?"

Snatching the necklace off the wall, I hurried down the stairs, which was a mistake. They wobbled under my feet, and I nearly fell. Spencer was standing outside the ruined front door, flashlight in one hand, his breath coming out in white clouds, his fingers tapping anxiously against one thigh.

"Hey," I said, yanking the door open. "What are you doing here?"

"Lester called me."

"What? How did he even get your number?"

"Um, he said you gave it to him? In case of emergencies? He said he heard a huge crash and a scream from your house. Said he didn't want to involve the police."

"Well, I don't know about the scream. I literally got back ten minutes ago. As for the crash..."

Moving aside, I gestured to the wreckage in the living room. Spencer shone his light in, and his mouth opened slightly.

"What happened?" he asked.

"There must have been some rotten supports," I said, not wanting to admit my own stupid mistake. "The loft collapsed into the living room."

"Thank god you weren't here when it happened."

A shout from outside made us both turn. Lester was hurrying up the driveway, waving his hands like he was on fire. One hand gripped an old rifle.

"Whoa," said Spencer, stepping back. "Hey, Lester, calm down."

"Where's Michelle?" Lester's voice cracked on the last syllable.

"Here," I said, moving forward. "Everything is fine, Lester."

"Why'd you scream?"

"I didn't scream. I only just got home from my trip."

"No, I heard it." Lester came to a stop on the porch, panting. "And the kids..."

Spencer and I exchanged a look. It was nice to be on the inside of one of those looks for once.

Lester's skinny chest heaved. Silver glinted in Spencer's flashlight beam – there was a chain around Lester's neck. I felt suddenly numb. The end of the chain was hidden by his blue button-down, but I was certain it contained an amethyst. That was where I'd seen it before.

"Did you put this in my house?" I held up the amethyst pendant. "It was hanging on my wall."

Lester and Spencer both stared, confused. But for once, my mind was completely clear. Everything made sense. The missing nails, the moved boxes, the locked doors, the time my phone was in the secret room. The necklace on the wall. All of it had been Lester.

"Did you do it?" I asked again, shoving the necklace in Lester's face.

"Hey," said Spencer, putting a hand on my arm.

I flinched but shook him off.

"Have you been in my house?" I enunciated each word clearly, staring right into Lester's eyes.

"Of course not," he said. His bewilderment was almost good enough to be real.

"So you didn't put my phone in the secret room?"

"Secret room?"

"I don't think he did it," said Spencer in a placating voice.

"Or steal my boxes of nails?" I continued, ignoring him. "A few weeks ago, they were in my kitchen cabinet, and then they were gone. Spencer was there; he saw it."

"Michelle, you put those nails in the upstairs bedroom."

"I... what?"

"You're talking about the day I came over to help with the countertops? You took the nails out of the cabinet and said you were moving them upstairs, since that's where you'd need them next."

He was right. I had totally forgotten.

"Okay, maybe," I said, breathless and desperate. "But I know this necklace came from him. He has one just like it."

Before Spencer could stop me, I reached out and yanked the chain around Lester's neck, convinced I would find a piece of amethyst at the end. But it wasn't amethyst. It was a round, slightly tarnished silver charm with the letter M engraved on it. M for Madeline – Lester's wife.

"Let go," Spencer hissed, and I dropped the pendant as if it had scalded me.

Angry red lines marked Lester's neck where I had pulled the chain. His eyes were watery and confused.

"I'm so sorry," I began, but Lester had already turned and marched away into the trees, shotgun dangling at his side.

"What the hell was that about?" Spencer asked once Lester was out of sight.

"I really thought he did it," I said, holding up my hands helplessly. "A lot of weird stuff has happened in this house, and it made sense that he was behind it all."

"You believed an 80-year-old man had been breaking into your house and stealing stuff? Come on."

"I... I don't..."

To my horror, a lump formed in my throat, and my nose stung. Not wanting Spencer to see me cry, I turned away and sniffed as quietly as I could. More than anything, I wished Chloe were there. That was the root of my trouble, wasn't it? Without her, everything was wrong. She had been my tether, and now I was drifting, aimless and alone.

A warm hand squeezed my shoulder, and for a second I let myself think it was Chloe, magically appearing when I needed her. Then Spencer spoke, and the spell was broken.

"What's wrong?" he said. "You've been kind of spacey lately. Like the thing with the nails."

"I forgot where I put them, that's all."

"That's not all. You didn't just forget – you were convinced they'd been taken."

Until that point, I had avoided it. I had made excuses. I had refused to acknowledge it, either to people like my dad or to myself. I wasn't sure what broke inside me at that exact moment. The collapse of the loft and the encounter with Lester had shaken me.

"I'm... having problems," I choked out as tears threatened to break loose. "I keep forgetting things."

"We're almost in our mid-thirties," said Spencer. "Forgetfulness comes with the territory."

"It's worse than that, like I'm losing big chunks of my memory, like I'm blacking out but somehow still walking around and doing things and talking."

I couldn't bring myself to tell him the worst parts – the glimpses of nonrecognition of people and places I'd known my whole life, and how easy it had become to believe that I'd witnessed things that never happened, like Lester wearing an amethyst necklace.

"Have you been sleeping well?" Spencer asked.

"No, but that's not what's causing it. And don't you fucking dare suggest it's stress-related."

"What do you think is causing it, then?"

If I told Spencer about my diagnosis, would he understand? He and I had gone to our fair share of college parties. One of the rare nights I clearly remembered involved the two of us heating up a whole bag's worth of marshmallows in a frat house microwave, resulting in a sticky mess we'd been too sloshed to clean up. After college, though, Spencer had left all that behind. He'd gotten a teaching job that he loved, and now the most he drank was a few beers on a Friday night or, on rare occasions, a couple of stronger drinks at a social gathering. Totally in control.

For Daniel and I, the party had never stopped. The friends we'd had since high school stuck together, hanging out almost every weekend, letting the alcohol flow freely. Even when we weren't at a party, it was typical to have two or three drinks with dinner. One Saturday, when Daniel was out of town, I awoke in my car in the middle of the night, sweaty and disoriented, to realize that I'd consumed an entire fifth of whiskey on my own and somehow managed to drive to the McDonald's down the street.

That had been the start of the blackouts.

"I'm not sure what's causing it," I said, not meeting his gaze. "But I've always been a poor sleeper, and nothing like this has happened before. I think...I think there's something wrong with me."

Spencer frowned. "Are there any other symptoms you've noticed?"

Other than the sleepwalking, insane dreams, and flashes of rage?

"I guess so. Itchy skin. Hair falling out."

"Jesus, Michelle. You need to go to a doctor."

"I don't have insurance, and I need to save my money for more important things."

"Like what?"

I gestured at the wrecked house.

"This house isn't more important than your health," said Spencer angrily. "My cousin Dana is a nurse practitioner; I'll see if she can do a free exam."

"No."

"Why not?"

Because I know exactly what's wrong with me, and no treatment will help.

"Because I just need more sleep and healthier food and to drink more water. And I think being in Indiana stressed me out, so now that I'm back, I'll be fine."

"You just said this wasn't stress-related."

"Maybe I'm wrong."

He looked like he wanted to keep arguing, but I didn't give him the chance.

"You should go," I said. "It's the middle of the night. I'll be fine."

"You and Monster should stay at my place tonight."

"I need to assess the damage here."

"Can't it wait until morning?"

"I'll be fine. See you later, Spencer."

With a brief wave, I went inside and locked the door behind me. When the sound of tires crunching on gravel faded, I wiped my eyes and got to work.

BY THE TIME SPENCER left, it was well after midnight. Much as I wanted to fix the mess I'd made, my back ached from the long drive, and my eyes were sore. Even so, I did what I could over the next hour. All the old stuff from the sound-proofed room was tossed unceremoniously in the rented dumpster. Then, arms throbbing from the effort and the scratches, I dragged out the wooden planks that had once been my loft.

My loft. Supposed to be my safe place, and now it was a pile of rubble.

With each trip outside to the dumpster, I glanced in the direction of Lester's house, though of course I couldn't see it through the trees. No amount of coffee or leftover chili could ever make up for what I'd done to him. What the hell had I been thinking?

At last, my body refused to move another inch, and I collapsed onto a cleared patch of floor. Without a blanket or a pillow, I still drifted off, my last thought that I'd forgotten to text my parents that I made it home.

Frantic barking woke me.

For a moment, I thought I was still in Indiana, and the neighbor's dog was barking. Any second now, Daniel would roll over and groan and say, "Why can't they make that thing shut up?" But these barks were familiar.

"Monster?" I said groggily, sitting up and rubbing my eyes.

The clock on my phone read 4:14 AM; I'd only been asleep for two hours. Monster was not beside me. Struggling to my feet, I peered around the corner, down the hall to the front door, which was shut. The barks were coming from that direction.

"Monster, how did you get out?" I groaned.

Flashlight in hand, I went outside and immediately headed toward the boulder with its apparently enticing hole. Monster wasn't there. The hole was so dark, pitch black, and I wondered if I could fit into it, just slither down into it like a snake.

More barking, this time from behind me. It was accompanied by a teeth-rattling shrill noise like nails on a chalkboard.

"Monster?" I called, walking back toward the house.

Above me, the moon was bright, glinting off my truck.

"Oh my god," I breathed.

Monster was *in* the truck. When he spotted me, his barking and whining intensified.

"Hold on just a second, buddy," I said, rushing into the house for my keys.

His nails had left scratches in the glass of the passenger window, and he'd had an accident on the seat. Not since early puppyhood had he had an accident, so I knew he'd been in the truck for a long time. As I cleaned the mess, I thought back through my actions since arriving. I had seen that the house was wrong, and I'd hopped out of the car, but Monster had been with me, hadn't he? Hadn't Spencer pet him? No, I was thinking of a different time.

Monster had been in the car for over 20 hours, with only a few breaks on our road trip home. We'd been together constantly since the move, and yet somehow I hadn't noticed his absence at bedtime.

"What the hell is wrong with me?" I muttered, scratching Monster's ears and hugging him around the neck. "I'm so sorry, buddy. I'm the worst mom ever."

Now that he was free, Monster seemed to have already forgotten about his captivity.

For once, I hoped that I would forget too.

CHAPTER 14

HAYDEN & SONS HARDWARE was completely empty on Saturday. The sign in the window said "Open", but I still hesitated before pushing on the door. It was unlocked, and the usual cheerful bell tinkled above. After repeated assurances from Hannah that it was okay, I'd brought Monster with me, though I was keeping a tight hold on his leash.

"Just a second!" called a voice from the back.

At the sound, Monster's ears perked up comically high. When Hannah came into view, carrying a box so large it obscured her face, Monster lunged at her excitedly, and I dug my heels in.

"Stop that," I scolded. "Sit."

He did so, albeit reluctantly. His tail wagged furiously, and he let out a frustrated whine.

"Is that my favorite good boy?" said Hannah, setting the box on the counter. "It is!"

"If I let him go, he's going to tackle you."

"Fine by me!"

The instant I released Monster's leash, he bounded forward. Hannah let out a peal of laughter as he reared up and put his paws on her shoulders so he could lick her face. I rolled my eyes. All that training, and he still hadn't learned not to jump. I couldn't be too mad, though, given what I'd put him through last night.

"Okay, okay," I said, finally pulling him back. "Let her breathe."

"Eh, breathing's overrated."

"You are such a spoiled dog, you know that?" I said to Monster. "Everyone loves you."

He looked up at me, tongue hanging, as Hannah scratched behind his ears. I rolled my eyes again.

"How was your Thanksgiving?" Hannah asked, straightening up. "You went home to Indiana, right?"

"Right," I agreed, though the term "home" didn't seem to fit anymore. "It was okay."

"Is that code for 'it sucked'?"

"Definitely."

"No wonder you're back so soon. In that case, my Thanksgiving was okay too."

We smiled in commiseration. I did not volunteer any more details, though. My trip to Indiana already felt like a faraway dream, sunk to the bottom of a deep well, and the last thing I wanted was to dredge it up.

"I ordered some more of that paint," Hannah said. "For your kitchen cabinets."

"Thanks, but I'm actually here for nails."

"Didn't you buy more right before Thanksgiving?"

"Turns out I need a whole lot more," I said with a sigh, tugging down my knit cap.

"Oh?"

Her face fell as I explained the collapse and all the resulting damage.

"That's beyond sucky," she said when I was done.

"It'll take me weeks to get back to where I was."

"Do you want some help?"

"Are you offering?"

"Sure." She gestured dryly at the hardware supplies. "I may know a thing or two about home repairs. I could even come today."

"What about the store?"

"One of the perks of ownership – I decide when we close. Besides, we don't get any customers right after holidays. I only came in to do inventory."

"Well, that's still important."

"I'll make you a deal. You help me with the inventory for an hour or two, and I'll spend the rest of the day helping out at your house."

"You'd really do that?"

She shrugged, and her cheeks went slightly pink. "Yeah. It actually sounds fun, and I like helping friends."

Friends. Just hearing it out loud made me warm inside, like I was finally laying my foundation here. It had been so long since I'd had someone I could rely on, aside from Chloe, and even that wasn't the case anymore.

"Great," I said, still smiling. "I like helping friends, too."

<hr>

THE NEXT MONTH GOT cold beyond all reckoning, even colder than was normal for a New Hampshire winter, according to Hannah. We hardly felt it, though. We were constantly on the go, working on the house or in the hardware store, or traveling the road in between with the heat and the radio cranked up. Why I had been too stubborn to ask for help before, I had no idea. The work was ten times faster and a thousand times more enjoyable with Hannah there.

One evening, after repainting the downstairs guest room and grouting the tiles in the bathroom, we built a fire outside, brewed a fresh pot of coffee, and watched the sunset through the trees.

"Hey, can I ask you something?" Hannah said, sounding un-characteristically serious.

"Sure."

"Why did you get divorced?"

Heat rose in my cheeks. Hannah's face was flushed too, her dark eyes fixed on mine, her hands clutching the tin mug. Anyone else might've gotten a brief, cold response to this question, but Hannah wasn't being judgmental or nosy, I could tell.

"Um," I said cautiously. "There were a lot of factors."

Hannah immediately waved a hand. "Never mind. I shouldn't have asked."

"It's okay. Really. I guess what it boils down to is, I didn't like who I was in the marriage. I didn't like the habits we'd fallen into. One day, I kind of woke up and thought, this isn't me, and I can't stand one more second of pretending."

"That makes sense," said Hannah, nodding.

"It may sound selfish, but all of that stuff that comes with marriage had started to feel like a chore, and I was sick of the obligations."

"Hey." Hannah bumped her foot against mine. "You're not selfish. It's never too late to discover yourself."

Especially after a life-changing and terrifying diagnosis.

How different would my life be if I'd been too cowardly to end my marriage? If I had ignored my symptoms and hadn't gone to the doctor? Instead of working outside in the cold, fresh air and making friends who accepted me, I'd be partying every weekend, blacking out, and dragging myself into the office each Monday with a heart full of dread. Even worse, Daniel had been mentioning starting a family. And even worse than that, I'd been considering it.

"A lot of the children I work with, their own parents don't recognize them anymore..."

My dad's words came back to me, more chilling than ever. What kind of parent would I have been when I could hardly take care of myself?

"Well, I'm sorry about the divorce," said Hannah. "But I'm glad you're here."

"Me too."

Between my short shifts at the hardware store – which I was actually getting paid for now – and my long hours reconstructing the loft, December passed in a blur. Nine days before Christmas, I finally installed the spiral staircase and climbed it for the first time.

"It's okay, boy," I said to Monster, who was whining up at me from the living room. "I'll get that main staircase fixed next so you can come up here with me."

The smells of new timber and wood stain in the loft were intoxicating. I closed my eyes and breathed deeply through my nose. Then, I thought I heard something.

"Shush, Monster, I'm trying to listen."

A scratching sound was coming from the far side of the loft. I had already knocked down the walls of one of the bedrooms, but I had left Simon's room (that's how I'd started to think of it) untouched. I told myself it was because the ceiling needed the support until I could put in a couple of columns, but really it was because I hated going near that room.

"It's probably a squirrel," I said, my footsteps thumping on the loft floor. "It better not be a raccoon."

I banged on the door, which I kept shut for reasons I couldn't explain, and yelled at whatever was in there to get out. There was a pause in the scratching, but it resumed once I fell silent. I put my ear to the door, hoping to at least get a better idea of what I was up against.

Something slammed against the door from the inside, making me gasp and leap away.

"You damn demon! What did you do to my children?!"

The voice was husky with emotion. There was a scrabbling noise and another slam.

"What'd you do to them?" the woman shrieked.

Desperately, I yanked on the doorknob, but all of the many locks were locked. Spotting a hammer on the floor, I grabbed it and began prying at the metal clasps and hinges just as the woman in the room let out an animal wail, followed by a third and final slam.

At last, the door burst inward, and I nearly tripped over a middle-aged woman on her knees. She was wearing a neat red dress with white buttons and a thin white belt. Disheveled dyed-brown hair with gray roots obscured her face. Her shoulders heaved with silent sobs. In her hands was something feathery and broken.

"Maybe it'll stop now," she said, making me jump again. "Maybe I fixed them."

"Fixed who?"

Her head snapped up, revealing red-rimmed eyes and flecks of blood on her cheeks and lips. "The ones we love."

"We?"

"Up, down, up down," she muttered, caressing the bird in her arms. "Left, right, left, right goes the beak. Then the bones go cold."

"I don't—"

"Mrs. Dennis? Wh-what are you doing?"

A boy in an orange shirt stood beside me in the doorway, blue eyes wide with terror.

"Don't let him see you, Kent," Shirley whispered. "Don't let him see you."

She held the limp bird up by one wing, and the boy screamed and ran. Simon's long tail feathers brushed the wood floor. One dark, doleful eye focused on me.

"Don't let him see you," Shirley hissed.

Gripping the bird's head, she twisted up, down, left, right.

The crack of the bird's neck woke me. Gray light coming through the window told me it was either early morning or early evening, though I was sure the sun had been shining high a minute ago. My neck twinged painfully as I sat up. For some reason, I'd been lying on the floor of Simon's room.

My head was unbearably itchy. I scratched and scratched, yet the itch wouldn't stop. When I pulled my hand away, a bloody clump of light brown hair clung to my fingers. I let it fall to the floor, where it landed on several long, deep gouges.

"LOTION. THAT'S ALL I need. Lotion and dandruff shampoo. And to stop talking to myself."

It was the week before Christmas, and I was walking along Mill Street, hoping that the grocery store was still open and that it had lotion. My skin and scalp were dry; that was the problem. I wasn't acclimated to such cold weather.

Across the street, an older couple was meandering down the sidewalk, talking in low voices and looking around like they were lost. Normally, I would've ignored them and kept going, but there was something endearing about the man's lined face and the woman's pink nose and the way they were holding hands.

"Excuse me," I called, waving. "Hi. Are you looking for something?"

They waved back with much more enthusiasm than I'd expected and hurriedly crossed the street to me, standing way too far inside my personal bubble. I was about to take a polite step back when the woman said, "We were hoping we'd run into you."

"You were?"

"Of course we were," she said, squeezing my arm. "You never gave us your exact address, and you weren't answering your phone, so we thought maybe you'd gone to do some shopping in town."

Their faces shifted into focus, and it clicked in my mind. "Mom? Dad?"

They exchanged a look, but their smiles didn't waver. I hugged them both and listened to my mom chatter away as I led them toward Beans & Brews to warm up. On the inside, I was deeply unsettled. My own parents had been right in front of my face, and I hadn't known them. I'd thought they were tourists from one of the nearby ski resorts.

Don't worry about it. It's like running into a coworker at the movie theater. Out of context.

But these weren't coworkers or acquaintances. These were my parents. I'd known them literally my entire life.

"Misha, your mom asked a question."

"Sorry, what?"

"Is the chai latte here any good?" my mom repeated.

"Oh, um, I don't know. I've only had coffee."

"I'll try it anyway. I'm feeling adventurous."

It was then that I noticed the strained quality of her voice and the tense set of my dad's jaw. I avoided his gaze as, in the background, my mom ordered a chai latte, a black coffee, and a mocha with extra whipped cream from a barista who kept glancing at the clock, no doubt ready to start her own holiday festivities. The whole scene felt like an upside-down, inside-out disorienting dream. Wait...maybe it *was* a dream. That would make a lot of sense. My dream about Shirley and Simon the day before had been incredibly real.

"Did I... forget something?" I asked as we waited for our drinks at a table by the window.

"Forget what?" my mom said, rubbing her hands together for warmth.

"Had we planned a visit? I wasn't expecting you."

"There was no plan," said my mom. "We hadn't heard from you in a while, so we wanted to come check on you."

"I was in Indiana a month ago," I pointed out.

"And we haven't gotten a call or text from you since, Misha," my dad said quietly. "We were worried."

"I've just been busy with the house."

"We understand that," my dad said in his peace-keeping-social-worker voice. "But you're living out in the woods all alone, and we need to hear from you occasionally so we know you're in one piece."

The barista arrived, heading off my retort about Chloe living in one of the most dangerous cities in the country. Whipped cream melted on my tongue, followed by the abrupt burn of hot coffee. My mom bombarded me with questions about my house and my job prospects and whether I'd made any new friends. My dad, on the other hand, remained silent, though I could feel his eyes on me.

"And we really need to know when you're coming for Christmas so we can have your room ready," Mom said. "We could always get you a ticket on our flight back tomorrow."

"I'm not sure..."

But she barreled on, hardly listening to my feeble attempts to tell her that I had no intention of coming home for Christmas. At Thanksgiving, I had felt so out of place, so on edge the entire time. The last thing I needed was another holiday filled with secret conversations and sidelong glances.

When it sounded like the barista was about to shatter the floor with her tapping foot, I ushered my parents back outside. The door closed and locked behind us.

"Why don't we continue this at your place?" my mom asked, pulling her puffy coat tighter.

"No."

They both stared at me. During our whole conversation, I had grown more and more wary. I had known this suggestion was coming, and I'd had my answer ready. I didn't want to hear my mom's comments about the smallness of the kitchen or my dad's questions about what type of security system I planned to get. My house was a sacred place for me and Monster only, and I did not want them intruding on it.

"I think you should go back to Indiana without me," I said.

My words hung in the frosty air for a full minute.

"We're not going to do that, Misha," my dad said, then cleared his throat twice. "We're worried you've been drinking again."

"I haven't."

"But we came all this way just to—"

"I don't want you here," I said, cutting my mom off. "I'm an adult, and I can take care of myself."

They protested a few more times, almost to the point of begging, but I wasn't listening. Leaving them next to their rental car, I hurried back down the street to my truck and, making sure they didn't follow me, headed home.

By the time I got there, I was half-convinced those people hadn't been my parents after all.

CHAPTER 15

M: Will you also grab another box of the flooring nails?

H: Didn't I bring you a box last week?

M: I guess I ran out.

H: Ok, I'll get those and the wood filler and head your way.

SIGHING, I SHOVED MY phone back into my pocket. I was on my knees in Simon's room, examining the scratches I was sure I'd already buffed out. The list of things left to do for the house was getting smaller and smaller. In the few days since Christmas, I had finally fixed the main staircase and installed a sturdy rail, put a last coat of paint on the cabinets and front door, and applied weatherproof sealant to the new back deck. Aside from the crack in the glass wall, the ground floor was nearly complete. It was the upper floor that continued to give me trouble.

During my busy high school and college years, I often had lengthy dreams about getting up in the morning and preparing for school, dreams that were so vivid I could taste the coffee in my to-go mug and feel the straps of my backpack digging into my shoulders. Then I would wake up for real to find that I hadn't done any of those things. In that same way, I had played out the scene of fixing these scratches a dozen times, only to return to Simon's room and find them still there.

Not only that, but I had made plans to knock out the walls at least once a week for the last three months. Somehow, I always got distracted with other, more urgent matters. Today, though, I was determined to get it done, and I had invited Hannah over to help. With her there to keep me on track, it would get taken care of.

"Time for a walk, Monster," I said when I went downstairs. "Hannah and I will be busy for a while, so we need to go now."

Recognizing Hannah's name, his tail wagged ferociously. Sometimes, I thought he liked Hannah more than me. Not that I was bitter about it.

We went out the front door, since the sealant on the back deck was still curing. It would take Hannah at least twenty minutes to arrive, so Monster and I set off on the path past the old stone well and toward Lester's house. At this point, the dark shape fluttering on the edge of my vision was a regular occurrence, so regular that I'd considered getting my eyes checked. I didn't bother looking closer, because I knew it would be gone when I did.

"No, Monster," I said sternly as he veered toward Lester's house. "Stay by me."

Through the trees, I could see that his house was dark and still. No old records playing. No Lester shuffling around the yard with a cup of coffee and his toolbox.

He and I hadn't spoken since I accused him of breaking and entering. Whenever Monster and I took a walk, I kept an eye out for him, and I saw him every once in a while, but I didn't know how to talk to him after how I'd treated him. It was kind of the same with Chloe. We had forged a tentative peace via text on Christmas, yet it felt like something between us was irrevocably broken. She was planning to fly up for a visit at the end of January for my birthday, and I wasn't sure if I felt more excited or anxious. Chloe and I must have been on the same wavelength, because my phone buzzed with a text from her.

C: What are your NYE plans?
M: Nothing really. Probably just make pasta and watch Rear Window.
C: Booooooooring
M: It's tradition!
C: You should at least go out for like an hour near midnight. Maybe you'll meet a hot & mysterious stranger to kiss.
M: "Go out"?
M: You know I live in the middle of the woods, right?
C: There's got to be a bar somewhere close by.

This suggestion from Chloe further confirmed that my parents hadn't shared their suspicions with her. Like me, they were doing their best to protect her from it.

M: Nah, I'm a homebody now.
C: Then invite people to your house!!
M: Maybe

My phone buzzed again, this time with a message from Hannah.

H: Here! Come help me unload?

"Shit," I muttered. I had gotten so caught up that I'd forgotten she was coming. My fingers flew across the screen.

M: On a walk, back in five minutes. Sorry!

"Monster!" I called.

His head jerked up from the mushroom he'd been sniffing. With a goofy grin, he ambled up to me, and we headed toward the house. As we walked, I noticed that his fluffy tail was matted. When was the last time I'd given him a bath and a good brush?

Sounds like I have a plan for New Year's Eve after all...

"I THINK IT'S A great idea."

"Seriously?"

"Of course!" Hannah sat back on her heels, wiping her forehead with her sleeve. "You've been here for, what, three months now? And the only people you know are me and Spencer."

"Almost four, actually. And I met your other friends – Francesca and, uh..."

"Reuben. They don't count, since you only met them once."

"Does the barista at Beans & Brews count?"

"Do you know her name?"

"Uh....."

"Then definitely not."

"Lester?"

She laughed and shook her head, curls bouncing.

For the last half hour, Hannah and I had been in Simon's room, trying once and for all to get rid of those damn scratches. Very carefully, we had been filling each gouge with wood filler and wiping away the excess. However, the scratches were so deep that I knew I'd probably end up having to use a sander.

A few minutes ago, I had made the mistake of mentioning Chloe's suggestion for a New Year's Eve party, and Hannah had latched onto it at once.

"There's not enough time to plan," I said as I redid my pony-tail. "New Year's Eve is in two days."

"That's plenty of time. It's not like you're planning a formal sit-down dinner for a hundred people. It can be as casual as you want it to be."

"It would take me at least a month to get this house par-ty-ready."

"What are you talking about? The downstairs is pretty much done."

"Yeah, but..." I gestured at the scratches and the busted win-dow frame. "What about all this?"

Hannah pursed her lips. "Did you have one of those moms that cleaned the baseboards before having company over?"

"Maybe. So?"

"So, nobody will even come up here. The party will be down-stairs and maybe outside at the fireplace."

"But what if—"

"I'll even get you a fancy velvet rope to block off the stairs if that will help."

Silence fell between us as Hannah gave me a moment to consider. Turning back to the task at hand, I filled another scratch, then gave up, pulling off my work gloves and dropping them on the floor. The idea of spending another holiday alone hadn't seemed sad until now.

My lonesome Christmas had been perfectly fine – Monster and I had gone on an extra-long walk, then retreated inside to watch the snow fall. I had made a grilled cheese and tomato soup, curled up on my new comfy couch, and watched White Christmas. It was the one Christmas movie that Chloe and I always made a point of watching together. Feeling her absence like a black hole at the other end of the couch, I had turned the movie off halfway through.

Now that I really thought about it, maybe it hadn't been that great after all.

"Okay," I said. "But I don't want any more than ten people, including me, you, Spencer, Reuben, and Francesca. Five more people max."

"No problemo," said Hannah, grinning. "Sorry. I'm just excited!"

"And I'll need help with food and stuff."

"I'll call in the troops. Francesca makes great apps, like spinach artichoke dip, mini mushroom tarts, all kinds of yummy stuff. And I have a pretty awesome recipe for strawberry champagne cupcakes."

I was already a little regretful and overwhelmed, and Hannah must have sensed it, because she put a hand on my knee.

"Hey. It'll be fun, I promise. No stress. You just focus on finishing the downstairs, and we'll take care of the rest."

We soon abandoned Simon's room and the planned demolition and went down to the kitchen for coffee. I noticed Hannah peering out at the deck, frowning.

"Something wrong?" I asked, handing her a mug.

"Did you put the sealant on the deck?"

"Yeah, yesterday."

"I thought we talked about this? The sealant won't cure in cold weather. I'm sorry, I must've forgotten to tell you."

I set my mug down and pinched the bridge of my nose. "No, you did tell me. I remember now. Shit, what am I going to do? It's probably all sticky."

"It's okay," said Hannah firmly. "We'll go into town and get sealant stripper and borrow my dad's power washer. That way, we can at least remove the stickiness before the party."

"I can't believe I did that. We really did have a whole conversation about it."

"Hey, come on. It's not like there's any damage done. As soon as warm weather arrives – you know, in May – we'll get it all fixed up."

She didn't seem fazed, but I felt incredibly stupid and disappointed. Things had been better lately. My arms had mostly healed. I hadn't been scratching as much or forgetting as many things. Some small part of me hoped I was getting better, but this was proof that I wasn't.

After a quick trip to the hardware store and the Haydens' house, Hannah and I stopped at the grocery store for party supplies. My bank account was still healthy, but I felt silly buying all the chintzy New Year's decorations, nonetheless. When I picked up a pack of sparkly silver party hats, my stomach squirmed. The last time I'd worn one of these was at the party that finally convinced me I wanted a divorce.

Almost exactly a year ago, Daniel and I had gathered with all of our friends to celebrate New Year's Eve, and I'd gone into it already tipsy from day-drinking. Yet even with a solid level of alcohol inside me, I hadn't felt like my usual party self. My surroundings were suddenly unfamiliar, as were all the people perched on couches or doing shots.

What am I doing here? Who are these people?

Those thoughts were the only distinct memory I had from that point on. The next thing I recalled was waking up sprawled on the floor, my whole body wracked with pain and a new hardness in my heart.

This would be my first real party since that day, and I was determined that it would be completely different.

I put the sparkly hats back on the shelf.

———◦———

MY ARCHITECTURE SKILLS HAD not carried over into interior design, and I was hesitant to consult Chloe again, especially since I hadn't even told her about the party. On New Year's Eve

Day, I surveyed my living room with unease. It was decorated exactly how I wanted it – simple and cozy. But was it nice enough for a party? The few actual New Year's Eve decorations I'd splurged on – black, silver, and gold streamers, giant gold number balloons, and noisemakers for the big moment – looked oddly forlorn.

When Hannah arrived around 3, I was immensely grateful for the opportunity to get out of my own head. We put up a few more decorations she said she'd found in the store's back room ("Nobody would've bought them after today anyway"), stacked logs in the outdoor fireplace, and hung a string of starry lights over the newly stripped deck.

"See, it's looking more festive already," she said reassuringly. "Want to help me frost cupcakes?"

The frosting had champagne in it, so I abstained from tasting, which was hard when it got on my fingers.

What's the big deal? It's a quarter of a cup in the whole batch.

Spencer got there next, juggling several bottles of liquor and exclaiming over how beautiful the house looked.

It would be rude not to drink any. He spent a lot of money on that.

Shut up.

I looked around to find Hannah and Spencer staring at me, wide-eyed.

Shit, did I say all that out loud? No. Definitely not.

"What?" I asked.

"Stop it," Hannah blurted.

"Stop what?"

She leapt forward, grabbed my hands, and pulled them away from my itchy collarbone. Crescents of skin and blood tipped my fingernails. But I didn't want to stop. It felt so damn good.

Yanking free of her grip, I resumed scratching. Not just my chest, but my neck and my face and my scalp. Then, even that wasn't enough. My groping fingers found a flap of skin, and I pulled. Hannah shrieked and covered her eyes. Spencer turned away, heaving. My flesh peeled away in long strips, only it wasn't flesh at all, it was feathers, light as air, spiraling to the floor in droves. Every inch of me was raw, and it felt—

"Happy New Year!!!"

Hannah's glass clinked against mine, startling me. Around us, couples were kissing and others were whirling their noisemakers. On my small TV, enormous crowds cheered and waved to the camera. Outside, a dark shape flitted past the glass wall.

"Are you okay?" Hannah asked.

"Why do I have this?" I demanded, shaking my mostly empty champagne flute.

"Um, you asked for it?"

"I don't drink."

"But you've had, like, a few drinks already."

"No, I haven't."

She gave a shaky giggle, clearly not sure whether I was joking or not. I dropped my glass on the rug, where the small remnant of champagne fizzed out. People were staring now. People I didn't know. People with too-large, too-dark eyes and pointed mouths. Where was Spencer? Where was Francesca?

"Who are you?" I cried.

"Okay, no more alcohol for you tonight."

I turned to Hannah, ready to protest, but she wasn't there. Instead, there was a woman who looked similar to her, yet definitely different in ways I couldn't explain.

"You're not real," I said, standing abruptly. "This isn't real. None of this is real!"

As I ran for the back door, my feet caught on the rug, and I fell face-first. My head slammed into the wood floor, and the world darkened.

Chapter 16

THE FOREST SHIVERED IN a cold wind that blasted against my cheeks, waking me. I was facedown on the ground, a pine needle stuck to my chapped lip. When I pried it loose, there was blood on it. My lip had split open from the fall. Rolling onto my back, I immediately noticed how bright the stars were.

"Cygnus," I muttered hoarsely, pointing up at the constellation.

Nearby, a river rushed and tumbled, but it didn't sound like my river, and these waving treetops weren't mine either.

My head swam as I sat up too abruptly. The whole world tilted, and my stomach heaved. Now, this was familiar. Barefoot in a place I didn't recognize, alcohol on my breath, throwing up. It was coming back to me – the New Year's Eve party, deciding that one drink wouldn't hurt, kicking my shoes off and dancing with Hannah. But how had I gotten out here? And where *was* here?

The path to my left seemed vaguely familiar, but I was still convinced that these weren't the woods near my house. The stars were too bright, the water too loud, the trees too tall.

"Monster?" I called, hoping against hope that he would appear, fluffy tail swishing, to lead me back home.

A giggle and a rustling bush made my head snap around.

"Monster?" I said again, quieter, knowing in my heart that it wasn't him.

"Don't laugh."

It was a young voice. That should have relaxed me, but instead it stole my breath. Another giggle shot a chill up my spine.

"Stop it, Sharon!"

"I told you we shouldn't have brought her," said another voice, also young.

"Well, we couldn't leave her at home with... you know. Come on."

From behind the bush, three small figures emerged. The tallest, a boy, carried a hefty flashlight in one hand and a shovel in the other. Next came a girl, maybe eight or nine, with long hair and a box in her arms. The third couldn't have been more than four, and she followed her siblings on unsteady feet. They walked right past without so much as glancing at me.

Without knowing why I was doing it, I walked behind them. Their silhouettes against the boy's flashlight beam bobbed up and down with each step. The middle girl began humming softly.

"What song?" asked the youngest.

"Sh," the boy scolded. "Quiet, Sharon."

"It's called All Things Bright and Beautiful," said the middle girl. "It's a church song."

"You be quiet too, Sylvia," the boy snapped. "Do you want her to hear us?"

They all fell silent, aside from Sylvia's humming. At a large elm tree, they stopped. I stopped, too, holding my breath. Without speaking, Sylvia set the box on the ground and took the flashlight from her brother, aiming it at the base of the tree, where there was a stretch of earth between two large, gnarled roots. The boy started digging, grunting each time the blade struck the ground. Sharon stood solemnly to one side, and I realized that she too was holding something.

Before long, there was a hole large enough for the box to fit neatly inside. Sylvia put it there, and her brother covered it with a mound of dirt.

"Okay, Sharon," he said. "Bring the rock."

Little Sharon moved forward, and I saw why she'd been walking so strangely. In her small hands, she held a large, flat rock. There appeared to be drawings or carvings on the rock, but I couldn't tell what they were. After setting the rock on the mound of dirt, she stepped back to join her siblings. The three of them held hands, swaying gently.

"We'll miss you, Simon," said the boy.

"We love you, Simon," said Sylvia.

"Bye, Simon," said Sharon.

A sudden shriek made all four of us jump. The siblings moved closer together, holding onto each other, as a tall shape emerged from the shadows, barreling toward the elm tree.

"Mama?" said Sharon, her sweet voice barely audible over the woman crashing through the undergrowth.

"Get behind me," said the boy, standing protectively in front of his sisters.

"You," the woman panted, grabbing the boy's arm and yanking so hard that he cried out. "You demon."

"No, mama, it's me! Simon!"

"What are you doing out here? Why did you bring the girls here?"

"We were burying the bird, mama," said Sylvia. "That's all."

With a high-pitched wail, the woman grabbed Sylvia's hair and dragged her away from the tree. Little Sharon, who had been clinging to her sister, fell and scraped her knee on a tree root. The boy beat against his mother's side, screaming for her to let Sylvia go.

"That devil bird is dead, and he still has a hold on you!" the woman moaned. "What have you done with them? Where are my children?"

"We're right here, mama!" gasped Sylvia, trying to wriggle free.

"Now he's got all your souls. All my babies... all my babies are gone."

The woman, Shirley, collapsed to the leaf-strewn ground, weeping and clawing at her face. Sylvia, who had fallen beside her, sat up and let out a blubbering sob, clutching her head. Yet in spite of everything, she then placed a comforting hand on her mother's shoulder. Simon returned to the tree, where Sharon was crying over her cut knee, and picked her up, trying to soothe her.

"We're not gone, we're here," said Sylvia gently, stroking her mother's back. "Me and Sharon and Simon."

At the sound of the name, Shirley let loose a bloodcurdling cry. Leaping to her feet, she grabbed Sylvia's arm in one hand and Simon's in the other, her nails digging in so hard that beads of blood appeared on their pale skin. The children tugged and begged, but she wouldn't release them.

"You won't get away this time," she hissed. "You'll give me my children back. You'll tell me where they are if I have to starve it out of you."

With incredible strength, she dragged her three children into the trees, their shouts and scuffles echoing back to me for a long, long time.

Once the screams had faded and the forest had settled back into its usual quiet rhythm, I approached the old elm tree. It was the same tree that I had woken up at the base of on that first night of camping, with the bloodstain and the ants.

"She killed the bird," I said, staring up into the stark, bare branches, "thinking it would make the children normal again. But it didn't."

And then she had put the "imposter" kids in the hole to starve them until they revealed the locations of her "real" kids. But what about the soundproof room and the poem etched into the ceiling there? Perhaps Shirley herself had slept in that room, where she wouldn't be able to hear her children calling for help, trying to trick her into releasing them.

Simon is the devil's eyes
Simon turns them all to lies
Simon seeks the world above
Simon takes the ones you love.

"Simon," I said, kneeling in the freshly dug earth. "What do you want?"

Now that I was closer, I could see what was painted on the rock. There was a childish depiction of a bird, with beady eyes, one misshapen wing, and four thin feathers sticking out of the top of its head. Below that was a drawing of a cross with three hearts surrounding it. Etched clumsily into the stone were two words.

Simon Forever

With one finger, I traced all the lines and curves of the letters. "Up, down, up, down. Left, right, left, right."

I clamped a hand over my mouth, and then I heard a noise coming from underneath the mound – frantic scratching. *Oh my god, they buried him alive!* As the realization hit me, I tossed the decorative rock aside and shoveled dirt away with my hands. Finally, my fingers hit the lid of the box, and I ripped it away.

Inside lay Simon, or what was left of him – fragile bones and clumps of brown and black feathers.

"I'm too late."

Even so, I removed the skeleton from the box and laid it gently on the ground. The hollow bones rattled against each other like a windchime, and the empty eye sockets gazed unseeingly at the too-bright stars. More than anything, I wanted Simon to be alive. If I could undo what Shirley had done, if I could reverse the madness, maybe Simon and I could both survive.

My forefinger and thumb closed around the small, brown beak. Using it, I nodded the skull up, down, up, down, like

Shirley had done when she'd snapped his neck, but gently. Then I made him turn left, right, left, right. Releasing the beak, I lined my fingers up with the wing bones, stroking them from base to tip twice, willing warmth into them. Lastly, I ran my fingers down the rib cage, all the way to the tips of the talons.

Cupping the body in my hands, I prostrated in a child's pose, my nose pressed to the dirt.

"Please, Simon, live. Stay with me."

A few minutes later – or it could've been longer – something sharp sliced my finger. Raising my head, I saw that my hands were now empty, and a great, dragonlike bird stood before me, its beak tipped in blood from the finger it had just nipped.

"Simon," I breathed. "You're alive. You're here. With me."

Those fathomless black eyes seemed to say, *And I'll stay with you. Forever.*

PART THREE: MOLTING

"...be still; don't struggle so like a wild, frantic bird, that is rending its own plumage in its desperation ."—Jane Eyre

CHAPTER 17

"HEY. WAKE UP."

It was so dark when I opened my eyes that I wondered whether I'd opened them at all. Then a crack of lightning illuminated the back deck and the trees beyond. I was on the couch, wrapped tightly in a soft blanket, with no idea how long I'd been there or what time it was.

"Michelle." Spencer was standing over me, a crease between his brows. "Hellooo."

"I'm up," I said, swinging my legs over the side of the couch.

"Finally. I didn't want to leave without saying goodbye."

"Leave?"

I noticed how empty the room was. And how clean. Hadn't there been a party here? Or had I imagined the whole thing?

"Everyone else left before the storm hit, but you were out cold," Spencer explained. "How do you feel?"

"Fine, I guess. What time is it?"

"A little after two."

"What? But what about the countdown?"

"You missed it."

"That's what I get for drinking again," I said without thinking.

"What do you mean?"

"I just haven't had a drink in a while. I guess it got to me."

"Were you drinking in the bathroom or something? Out here, I only ever saw you with a mug of coffee. Reuben mocked you relentlessly about it. Don't you remember?" He watched me as I tried to process this piece of information. "Oh. You really don't remember."

"No," I admitted. "The last thing I remember is tripping and hitting my head on the floor."

And watching three children bury a bird in the woods.

"You tripped?"

"Yeah, right there." I pointed. "Right after the countdown and the... the champagne."

I could tell from his expression that everything I'd said was wrong.

"Michelle, you were asleep before midnight."

"No, I distinctly—"

"You were on the couch next to Hannah, and you just conked out. We were going to wake you up for midnight, but she told us not to, said you'd been working hard and needed the rest. So we kept quiet. Didn't even use those." He gestured to the noisemakers. "Then the storm rolled in, and everyone headed home. I told Hannah I'd make sure you were okay before I left."

My lips pressed together, and my bare toes tapped relentlessly against the rug. "I didn't go outside?" I asked. "I didn't leave the house at all?"

"No," he said, drawing the word out. "You were on that couch the whole time."

"Where's Monster?" I said suddenly, my heart rate accelerating, half-expecting him to say *"Who?"*

"I put him upstairs in that bedroom. All the noise and people were overexciting him."

Jumping up, I strode to the spiral staircase and took it two steps at a time, nearly twisting my ankle. Spencer was still talking, but I didn't know or care what he was saying. The loft looked strange and lopsided with one room intact and the rest of it wide open. Why hadn't I torn down those walls yet? Hannah and I had meant to the other day, but we hadn't, because...because why?

When I reached the door, I found all of the locks shut tight. A scratching noise came from inside.

"Why the fuck is this locked?" I demanded of Spencer, who had followed me.

"I didn't lock it, I swear."

Pushing past him, I grabbed a hammer from my toolbox and returned to the door.

"Whoa," Spencer said. "Don't you have the keys?"

"They're not my locks. Move out of the way!"

"Can't you just take the hinges off?"

"Back up, Monster," I called, hoping he'd understand. "I'm coming in."

One, two, three times I smashed the hammer into the locks and the knob. They finally gave way, and I nudged the door open with my foot. At first, I thought the room was empty. Then I saw Monster cowering in a corner, looking far smaller than he had any right to look.

"Buddy?" I said, approaching him. "What's wrong?"

He was staring at me like he had no idea who I was. I held out my hand for him to sniff, and he backed away like I'd tried to hit him. Long, bloody scratches slashed across his snout. I rounded on Spencer.

"What. Happened."

"Nothing!" His eyes traveled to the scratches and back to me. "They don't look very deep. Maybe we can—"

"Get out. Please."

"Let me help you."

"We don't want your help."

After a moment, he left, and I heard the front door open and close. I sat on the floor, making no noise and no sudden movements, and eventually Monster crawled over and laid his head on my lap. Although I was fairly certain I was going crazy and having vivid hallucinations, I could always be sure that

Monster trusted me, and that I would do anything to protect
him.

———◄O►———

HOURS LATER, AFTER A long, harrowing, and expensive trip to
the nearest emergency veterinarian, Monster and I returned
home. He was on mild painkillers, so I had to lift him out of
the truck, which I was barely able to do. With trembling arms, I
set him gently on the frosty gravel. It was barely 9 AM, and still
cloudy; the woods around us were silent in that post-storm
kind of way, everything waiting to come out of hiding.

"Come on, buddy," I said, clipping Monster's leash to his
harness. "Time for your antibiotics."

He was unsteady on his feet, and I had to guide him all
the way inside. A fat squirrel darted across our path, and he
didn't show the slightest interest. Tears pricked my eyes as
he stumbled up the steps to the front door like a drunk. I
struggled to fit the key in the lock, dropping it with a clatter
when my phone rang.

It was Chloe.

"Hey, can I call you back?"

"Is everything okay?"

"I just got back from taking Monster to the vet."

"On New Year's Day?"

"It was an emergency," I explained as I finally managed to
get my key into the lock and opened the door.

"Shit, no wonder you sound upset. Is he all right?"

"He will be. He's a little drugged up at the moment. Hold on
a second."

Setting the phone on the kitchen counter, I peeled a ba-
nana, broke off a chunk, and shoved the antibiotic pill inside.
Monster sniffed it unenthusiastically. Finally, he accepted it.
But he only ate the banana, and the pill dropped onto the floor.

"Fuck. Please, just take it."

This time, I smeared the pill with peanut butter, and he gulped it down. I washed my hands and picked up the phone again.

"Sorry."

"What was that all about?"

"Ever tried to get an animal to take medicine?"

"Yikes. So, what happened to him?"

"I had some people over last night—"

"You did? Yay! Sorry. Continue."

"My friend Spencer locked Monster in an upstairs bedroom without asking me, and when I went to let Monster out, he was huddled in a corner with these bad scratches on his snout."

"Scratches? From what?"

"The vet said they looked like talon marks. My best guess is that an owl or a raven got in somehow, saw Monster, panicked, and took a swipe at him as it tried to fly away."

"Oh my god, that's crazy."

"I guess I'll never *really* know." I slipped out of my shoes and collapsed onto the couch. "Anyway, enough about that. I get mad whenever I think about it. What's up?"

"Oh, yeah! I wanted to tell you that they finally approved my time off."

"Time off?"

"From work."

"You got a job?"

"Same job. Coffee shop, remember?"

"Right," I said. "Time off for what?"

A beat of silence. "For your birthday? I was going to come visit you for a week. But if you're too busy—"

"No, sorry. I'm just distracted. I'm excited for you to come!"

"Are you sure?"

"Of course! Have you booked your flights yet?"

"No, that's what I wanted to ask about. The best airport is like an hour away from you, and..."

For another fifteen minutes, I listened to her talk about her visit, barely responding as she worked out dates and times and other details. The whole time, my eyes remained on Monster, who had retreated to his new bed and fallen fast asleep. To reassure myself that he was breathing, I concentrated on the rise and fall of his side. At the end of the call, I reminded Chloe to bring outdoor boots and warm clothes. Then I hung up and let out a long sigh.

When and why had we agreed to this visit? At the time, it must have sounded enjoyable, but now I was dreading it. Her plans felt almost as intrusive as when my parents had shown up unannounced.

No. That didn't really happen, Michelle. It was a weird dream, nothing more.

After checking Monster's breathing again, I turned on lights, built a fire in the indoor fireplace, ate cold leftover pasta, and headed upstairs. There was one thing I was finally ready to take care of. It had been beating on the back of my brain the whole drive back from the vet, and I couldn't ignore it any longer.

It was time to destroy Simon's room.

The door was still ajar from when I'd kicked it open. Was that really only this morning? Dangling, the golden knob twinkled in the beam of my flashlight, as did the remnants of the locks. I flicked the light switch, and nothing happened, even though it had been working fine earlier, so I brought up a few of my portable lights and placed them strategically. My shadow hit the wall at two angles.

How sad it must have been for Simon to be locked in this small, dreadful room, the window taunting him with its pretty picture of the outside world, of freedom just beyond his reach.

Crossing the room, my shadows shifting, I looked out the window. All I could see were the silhouettes of trees leaning back and forth in the wind, and the dark shape of a bird landing on a nearby branch. I was now positive that the bird I'd been seeing all along was Simon, though I still had no idea what he was attempting to tell me or what he wanted from me.

Figure it out later. You have a job to do.

First, I removed the door and window frame, pried up the baseboards, and detached what remained of the locks. Then I covered the window with a tarp and laid dropcloths throughout the loft to catch debris. I had already had these walls checked by the electrician and plumber, and they also weren't load-bearing, so I knew they were safe to knock down.

Quickly checking to make sure Monster was still content, I grabbed my sledgehammer, gripping it tightly with both hands, and swung. Chunks of drywall flew, some of them pinging off my safety goggles. I knew I would need to remove the rest of it with my reciprocating saw, but I couldn't stop. Each hit was like a vent for one of my fears or frustrations – my anger at Spencer; my regret over yelling at him; my worry about Monster's injury; my dread of Chloe's visit; my embarrassment that I had forgotten about the visit.

When my arms couldn't bear the weight any longer, I set the sledgehammer on the floor. Panting, I waved away a cloud of dust. Exhausted as I was, I had to admit that the sight of the partly demolished wall was satisfying. And there was something truly beautiful about the timing lining up with the start of the new year.

The house was almost complete. Soon, unlike Simon, I would belong here.

CHAPTER 18

ENERGIZED BY THE ADRENALINE of smashing those walls, I stayed
up all night cutting away the rest of the drywall and removing
the studs and plates. Then, I dragged the materials downstairs
and into the side yard. Some went in the dumpster, others in
the temporary storage shed that the police were still grudgingly
letting me use until I could rebuild the garage. Each time I
went outside, the well-below-freezing air cooled my sweaty
skin, making me shiver. Yet as soon as I went back in, I started
sweating again.

When the big pieces were gone, I cut away any remains before
sweeping the loft. By the time I was done, the light outside the
window had gone from pitch black to soft gray. The remnants of
the storm had finally cleared, leaving behind only a few streaks
of cloud. There was still a lot to be done, but exhaustion was
catching up to me. My arms ached from all the heavy lifting,
and I had to stop to catch my breath more frequently. Knowing
that the work would still be there after a few hours' sleep, I
descended the spiral staircase, casting one last look over my
shoulder at the wide-open loft.

Monster was still asleep, and I made a pallet on the floor
beside him, falling asleep with my hand on his paw.

It was astonishingly bright when I woke up and checked the clock. Almost noon. Monster was sitting up and gazing attentively out the glass wall at a cardinal on the deck railing. I squeezed his paw, and he leaned down to lick the back of my hand.

"Have you forgiven me for poisoning your banana?" I asked.

His suspicious side-eye said that he would probably never accept a piece of banana from me again.

"And your peanut butter?"

He licked his lips. Those were two words he definitely knew.

"Oh, so you still like it? Good thing, because it's time for more."

Groaning, I stood up. Every muscle in my body was sore from the stress and hard work of the day before. I slathered another antibiotic pill in peanut butter, and Monster accepted it. Then I scrambled a few eggs and brewed a pot of coffee. I was just about to step outside when a loud bang on the front door made me jump, sloshing a bit of coffee onto the wood floor.

"Damn it," I said as Monster let out a booming bark.

Whoever it was continued knocking forcefully until I undid the lock. It was Lester, looking and smelling like he hadn't bathed in weeks.

"Did you see him?" Lester said hoarsely the instant I opened the door.

"See who?"

"The bird. That damn bird. The one I told you about."

"Simon."

His face spasmed at the name. "I knew it. You've seen him, haven't you?"

"Of course not," I lied. "Didn't he die, like, fifty years ago?"

"I thought he was gone for good this time." Lester's cheeks were as hollow as his eyes. "I hadn't seen him in so long, and then you moved in, and I knew, I just *knew* it would happen again. I knew..."

He trailed off, rubbing his eyes so hard it must have hurt.

"Lester," I said soothingly. "Even if Simon hadn't died during all that stuff fifty years ago, there's no way he could have survived this long. The lifespan of a great eared nightjar is only twelve years. Besides, I saw a grave for Simon in the woods."

"You saw that?"

"Yes," I said, but I couldn't quite remember when or where. "Why would they make a grave for a bird that isn't dead?"

"It's empty." Lester's tortured gaze met mine. "I went to dig it up. After the storm. But somebody else already done it."

An image came to me of a bird carved into a rock and the words "Simon Forever". Was it something I'd actually seen before, or was I inventing it like I'd invented Lester's amethyst necklace?

"Maybe the storm softened the ground and the box came loose," I suggested.

And how did I know there was a box? Assumption?

"No bones," said Lester, shaking his head. "Lid closed, but no bones inside."

"Maybe a wild animal—"

"You be careful, young lady. Watch for the bird. Don't let him trick you like he tricked Shirley."

THE GROUND WAS STILL mushy from the heavy rains, yet there was also a thin layer of ice, so my boots crackled and squelched with every step.

"Are you sure you don't want to come?" I said to Monster, who was watching me from the deck.

He had followed as far as the stairs and refused to go any further. Although he seemed much steadier than he'd been last night, he was still a subdued version of his usual self. Part of me knew I should apologize to Spencer for exploding. It hadn't been his fault. How could he possibly have predicted a crazy bird attack? And was that even what had happened? The more I thought about it, the more unlikely it seemed.

I reached into my coat pocket only to remember that I'd left my phone inside to charge. I'd been carrying it with me less and less. Honestly, I didn't miss it.

I'll use this walk to compose the perfect apology message, I vowed to myself.

"If you change your mind, I'm going that way," I told Monster, pointing down the path to Lester's house.

His hesitant eyes flicked to the path and back to me.

"I won't stay gone long. Promise."

Placing my feet carefully so as not to slip, I headed along the trail. Since my conversation with Lester earlier, I had been straining to remember where I'd seen Simon's grave and the box inside. Obviously, I hadn't just invented it, because Lester had seen it too.

I also kept picturing the crude bird drawing and the words "Simon Forever" and occasionally a cross. For some reason, these images were linked in my mind with children. Something to do with children.

As I walked, meandering off the path, I scanned the bases of trees. If someone really had dug up whatever box Simon had been buried in, it would be easy to spot among the monotonous dead brown of the forest floor. But when I passed Lester's house, I began to think I'd never find it. I continued for another ten minutes before turning around, thinking it unlikely that Simon had been buried this far from his house.

Halfway between Lester's house and mine, my gaze fell on a towering elm, its gnarled roots jutting up from the ground. My hands went clammy. This was it. Crouching, I dug through the matted leaves and wet dirt, certain that underneath I would find a box and a large rock with a bird carved into it.

"Damn it," I said a few minutes later.

Having dug in between all the roots and come up empty-handed, I now stood beneath the tree, my hands freezing and my fingernails caked with mud. Then, a high-pitched and strangely familiar giggle made me turn.

"Sharon?" I said, not knowing where the name had come from.

"Hello? Is someone there?" The voice was soft and weak. I cocked my head, trying to figure out where it was coming from. I had a decent view of the yard, and there was nobody in sight.

"Where are you?" I called.

"Help! Please, help us!"

Without thinking, I ran, following the shouting voices until I arrived at the hole at the base of the boulder. There was no doubt about it – the voices were coming from down there. I reached once more for my phone to call 911 and found nothing but an empty pocket.

"Hold on, Sharon," said a female voice. "Someone will hear us soon."

Then came the sound of crying, pitiful and hopeless.

I tried to say, "I'm coming", but the words dried up in my throat. Instead, I sprinted to the house and returned with a flashlight and a length of rope. Tying the rope around the flashlight, I lowered it into the hole, lying on my stomach for a better view. Six feet down, the flashlight hit the bottom. Its beam revealed a small cavern, no more than twenty square feet. It was empty.

Crawling closer, I tried to see if there was a second area where the children might be, but the cavern seemed entirely closed off. And the voices had stopped.

Sharon. Sylvia.

It was like I knew them, but I didn't know how. At that same moment, I knew that they had died long ago. Or maybe just one of them had?

"I'm fucking losing it," I said, resting my forehead against the moist ground.

From the direction of the house came a sharp whine followed by whimpering. *Monster!* Jumping up, I hurried home, slipping a couple of times on mud and wet pine needles. Monster was still on the porch, pawing at the back door, his nails screeching against the glass.

"Hey, stop that," I said, wincing at the high-pitched sound. "What are you doing?"

At my approach, Monster's ears flattened on his head, and his muzzle pulled back in a snarl. I froze and held up my hands.

"Whoa. It's me, buddy. Only me."

The stitches on his snout had broken loose, and the cuts were bleeding again. He was reacting out of pain and fear rather than aggression, but I was still wary. I stood tall and made slow movements toward him. He shrank away but didn't snap at me, which I took to be a good sign.

"It's okay. Everything's okay."

But as soon as I got within a few feet of him, Monster darted around me and off into the woods, disappearing in the blink of an eye.

***

DARKNESS FELL, AND MONSTER was nowhere to be found. He knew these woods well by now, and he could take care of himself, but I worried that in his agitation he might slip into the icy river or even dig his way into the hole by the boulder. Before I gave up for the night, I blocked the hole as best I could with my metal toolbox, and I propped the back door open slightly in case he came home.

Note to self: install a dog door.

Small relief came from the fact that it was at least a clear night, and that Monster was bred for this kind of weather. As long as he stayed dry, he wouldn't be in danger of freezing.

To keep myself from drowning in anxiety, I worked on prepping the downstairs bedroom for Chloe's visit. When I tried to view the room through her eyes, I realized how dull it was — neutral color for the walls (maybe *too* neutral) and no curtains or decorations. Maybe during her stay, we could decorate together. She was much better at it than I was.

In the meantime, though, I put clean sheets on the queen-sized bed, which barely fit but gave the room a close, cozy atmosphere. Then I checked the hall bathroom and kitchen, making a list as I went, knowing I'd need to go shopping in Arden Woods sooner rather than later. The idea of leaving home, even for a few hours, while Monster was missing did not thrill me. But if he didn't come back soon, I'd have no choice.

Around midnight, I settled once more onto my pallet on the floor.

Note to self: maybe finally get your own bed, dumbass.

Even if I'd had a bed, though, I would've slept down there, in case Monster turned up.

For two hours, I watched the back door, willing him to appear. When it became clear that sleep wasn't possible, I paced between the kitchen and the glass wall, only stopping when I realized that my hand was making that strange motion again.

"Just do something," I commanded myself. "Anything."

The rich aroma of brewing coffee perked me up, and I prepared a mug with extra sugar and a bit of cocoa powder. Then I stood on the back porch for a few minutes, calling Monster's name, searching the shadows for his shaggy shape. When the cold got to be too much, I went inside, pulled the door mostly shut, and climbed the spiral staircase.

At the top, I froze. The mug slipped from my hands, shattering on the floor.

"This isn't possible."

Simon's room was back, its walls perfectly intact. Knowing and hoping that it might be my imagination, I ran across the loft, pressing my hands against the all-too-solid walls. The door was there, too, and all the locks that I could distinctly remember prying loose.

With a grunt of rage, I snatched my sledgehammer off the floor and swung. I didn't bother to put down tarps or wear my safety glasses or take any of the precautions I'd been so careful about last time. I just needed this room to be gone. I swung and swung, pushing past the ache in my arms, ignoring the tiny slivers of plaster that flew at me, slicing my face.

In the end, it was the cold that stopped me. I was suddenly shivering, my hands frozen to the hammer's handle, my breath coming out in white puffs. And then I realized that I was looking outside, not through the window, but through an enormous hole. A hole that I had made.

Around me, the walls of Simon's room had disappeared.

I dropped the sledgehammer, wincing as it landed a centimeter from my toes.

⸻ ◆ ⸻

"YES, I JUST WANT to know if a girl named Sylvia Dennis lived there back in the 70s. No, I'm not a relative, but – please? Shit."

I hung up the phone for the fourth time that day. There weren't a lot of children's homes in New Hampshire, and I had now called about half of them with no luck. Places like that never gave out private information, no matter what movies led people to believe. For the first one, I had tried lying and saying I was Sylvia's cousin, and the unimpressed receptionist had simply said "mm hm".

For the second children's home, I claimed to be Sylvia's long-lost sister. Unfortunately, *that* receptionist had an impeccable memory, was well aware of the Dennis murders, and basically told me to fuck off. After that, I opted to tell the truth. But I never got farther than "No, I'm not a relative".

Wearily, I eyed the remaining phone numbers on my list. Instead, I called Hannah.

"Oh, thank god, I'm so bored," she answered.

"Have you ever been to Waterside?"

"Um...yeah, a couple times I think, to go to parties at the lake in the summer. Why?"

"I just wanted to make sure it really exists, because I've been trying to find some information about a place there, and I'm having a hard time."

"Is this about Sylvia Dennis again?"

The way she said it made it sound like I'd been constantly bugging her with my quest to find Sylvia, though I was sure I'd only mentioned it once or twice.

"She lived at a children's home there in 1972," I said. "I found a picture, but that's it. I want to know what happened to Sylvia after she lived in that home. I've been calling all these other children's homes, thinking maybe she was moved, but they won't tell me anything."

"What can *I* do? I'm not exactly an internet sleuth."

I hesitated. Things had been a little tense between me and Spencer – and, by extension, Hannah – since New Year's, and I knew that what I was about to ask wouldn't help that. But I was desperate to find someone who could relate to what this house was putting me through.

"Can you talk to your grandpa? See if he remembers anything?"

"I told you, my dad doesn't want me talking to Grandpa about this."

"There's nobody else I can ask."

"What about Lester? Wouldn't he have kept tabs on Sylvia or even written to her after what happened?"

Yet another person who was avoiding me. "Lester doesn't know anything," I said, reasoning that it wasn't exactly a lie, since I wasn't sure what he did or didn't know.

Hannah sighed. "If you think it will help..."

"I do," I said quickly. "I really do."

"My dad's working in the store, so I'll go now. Call you soon."

When she hung up, I paced around the living room, knowing that I should be repairing that hole I'd made upstairs but unable to focus. There was something else I should be doing too, something important hovering at the edge of my brain, out of reach.

"Hello?" I said, snatching up the phone before the first ring ended.

"I talked to Grandpa." Hannah's voice was strange, like she couldn't quite believe what she was about to say. "He actually remembered clearly."

"Remembered what?" I asked breathlessly.

"When Sylvia turned 18, she moved back home, back to the A-frame."

"What?"

"Yeah. But here's the crazy part: she only lived there for a few months before she was taken to a psychiatric facility. After that, nobody knows what happened to her. She never came back to Arden Woods, though."

"She came back to this house... and she had a mental breakdown," I said slowly.

"Well, we can't know for sure—"

"Thanks, Hannah," I said and hung up.

So, it *was* the house that caused problems, not the people who lived in it. Three sane women – Shirley, Sylvia, and now me – had gone insane because of this house and whatever hold Simon had on it.

CHAPTER 19

THE DRIVE TO ARDEN Woods the next day was icy and unpleasant. Lost in my thoughts about Sylvia and Simon and the house, I drifted toward the edge of the road several times. The lack of sleep didn't help, either. I couldn't remember the last time I'd slept well, but last night had been particularly bad. Though I had patched up the hole in the wall as best I could, the cold air found its way inside. Out of firewood, I had spent the night huddling under blankets, clutching a fresh mug of coffee just to keep warm.

I needed supplies to repair the hole, but my main reason for going to town was that I needed help.

Not the kind of help my parents told me I needed. Not psychological help. Not yet, anyway. The help I needed was of a more supernatural variety. Everything that had happened – the voices, Monster's scratches, the phantom walls – had been caused by Simon, I was sure of it.

Do you even hear yourself? What the hell is wrong with you? How can a dead bird hurt you?

Haunting, said the Devil's advocate in the back of my mind. *Possession. Like with Shirley's kids. Maybe they weren't im-*

*posters; maybe they were possessed by Simon. And maybe I am
too.*

Since I'd had no luck tracking down Sylvia and getting her
help, I had to resort to other means.

Once I got closer to town, the roads cleared up. Even though
it was peak skiing season, I had no trouble finding a parking spot
along Mill Street, right across from the New Age shop with its
array of crystals winking in the wintry sunshine. Old Michelle
would've laughed at the very idea of stepping foot in a place like
this. She hadn't believed in spirits or hauntings or herbalism or
any of that hippie junk. But Old Michelle hadn't seen what I'd
seen.

Even though the hand-written hours posted in the window
said the store was open, I feared otherwise. In a town this small,
many places shut down for weeks or even months over the
holidays. Just in case, I tried the door, and it was unlocked.
Tentatively, I pushed it open and was hit with a strange yet also
familiar smell – vanilla mixed with pine and a hint of orange.

"Hello?" I called. "Are you open?"

"Yes, just a moment, please!"

A woman appeared from a back room. She was not at all what
I had expected. In fact, her appearance was almost a parody of
normalcy. She wore unflattering mom jeans, a pink sweatshirt,
and white tennis shoes. Her iron-gray hair was cut short, and
reading glasses hung on a delicate silver chain around her neck.

"Oh," she said in surprise. "Good to see you again."

"I'm sorry?"

"I guess if you're back so soon, that amulet must not have
taken care of the problem."

"The amulet?"

She gave me an odd look, but then the store phone rang, and
she turned to answer it. As she spoke to the person about the
types of cone and stick incense they carried, I looked around.
The shop was small and crammed with shelves, every surface
occupied. There were pewter figurines of fairies and dragons,

plastic bins of brightly colored gemstones, and candles in every size, color, and scent. Beneath the candles was a sign that stated, *"Candles are hand-poured in shop"*.

One shelf contained a couple dozen books. Reading the spines, I selected one titled "Omens & Curses: How to Tell Them Apart". On the cover was a campy image of a half-naked pin-up girl leaning provocatively over a Ouija board. I immediately put the book back.

Just then, I heard the phone click back into the receiver, and I returned to the counter.

"Hi," I said quickly. "This might sound weird, but could you tell me what you know about protection from the supernatural? Like hauntings or possessions."

Her frown deepened. "So, I'm right? The amulet didn't work?"

"What amulet?"

My voice rose with frustration, because I had obviously been here before but had zero memory of it.

"The amethyst pendant on the silver chain," said the woman, setting her glasses on her nose and staring at me over them. "Amethyst is a strong protector, though maybe not strong enough in this case."

The pendant in the soundproof room, the one I'd accused Lester of putting there, it had been mine all along. I'd come into this shop weeks ago, bought the pendant, taken it home, hung it in that room, and I didn't remember a single second of it. My head throbbed, and I pressed my fingers into my temples.

"Maybe protection isn't what you need," said the woman. "How about something to help with your memory?"

"You can do that?"

"I can certainly try. Wait here."

My headache grew steadily worse. I tried to distract myself by watching passing cars, by further examining the shelves, by aimlessly scrolling through Instagram, but none of it helped. I wanted nothing more than to go home and sleep, but if there was anything in this store that could improve my memory, I needed it.

"Here we are."

The woman plunked an array of items down on the counter.

"Gingko biloba tea," she said, holding up a paper bag. "From our own greenhouse. I've also got turmeric root, lemon balm, a quartz bracelet, and some lapis lazuli. Take your pick; it's on the house."

"Really?"

She looked over the top of her glasses. "I like my customers to be satisfied, and that pendant didn't do the trick."

"Okay, thanks. I'll take the tea."

She folded the top down on the brown paper bag but didn't hand it to me yet.

"I'm sorry, but I have to get going," I said, reaching for the bag.

"Of course."

Still, she didn't give it to me. She was looking down at her wrinkled hands with a hard-to-read expression. What exactly had I told her the last time I was here? Then, she shook her head slightly and slid the bag across the counter.

"Thanks," I said, taking it and turning to go.

"Michelle?"

Pausing with one hand on the door, I looked back at her. She looked different somehow. Not like a frumpy hippie grandma, but like a person who *knew* things. Her olive-green eyes locked on mine.

"Please be safe."

Back outside, squinting in the glare of the sun, I hesitated, not sure where to go next. The unnerving visit with the New Age shop woman had left me out of sorts. To give myself a little longer to remember my other errands, I walked to Beans & Brews and ordered a mocha to-go.

As I waited for the drink, I pulled out the paper bag of tea. It was very unofficial-looking, with no label or shop logo stamped on it. Unfolding the top, I sniffed. Notes of ginger and lemon tickled my nose, but underneath was something strange and almost putrid. Wrinkling my nose, I closed the bag again and stuffed it in my pocket.

"Groceries," I said when I stepped outside. "I was going to get pasta and dog food..."

No, that wasn't right.

"Hello? Michelle?"

I turned to see Hannah trotting along next to me, her dark curls bouncing, her expression concerned.

"Oh, hey," I said, suddenly recalling my real reason for coming to town. "I was about to grab some groceries and then come by your store."

She stopped walking, looking confused. I stopped as well.

"What?" I asked.

"I know we haven't known each other long," she said. "So, I'm sorry if this comes across weird or creepy or like it's not my place, but... where the hell have you been?"

"What do you mean?"

"I haven't seen or heard from you since the New Year's party, except for when you asked me to talk to my grandpa about Sylvia Dennis. I've been worried."

"Why would you be worried?"

"I've been texting and calling for three weeks, not like a stalker, just a normal amount, and you haven't responded once."

"Oh." I patted my pockets, but my phone wasn't there. "Wait, did you say three weeks?"

"Yeah. Since New Year's."

"It's already been three weeks? I mean," I said in an attempt to cover myself, "it just doesn't seem that long."

"Well, it has been." She sighed. "I'm not trying to be clingy. But Spencer told me what happened to Monster, and I wanted to check up on both of you. Is he okay?"

"Monster? Yeah, he... Actually, I don't know if he's okay." I shrugged. "He ran away yesterday."

Had it been yesterday, though? I had also thought yesterday was early January, but apparently not.

"What?" said Hannah. "I can't believe it. That's terrible. I don't get it – why would he run away?"

"I think whatever gave him those scratches came back and freaked him out. I tried to calm him down, but..."

"He'll come back. Breeds like that are smart – too smart, sometimes – and I've seen how loyal he is to you."

"Yeah, but what if he's..."

Hannah put a hand on my arm and squeezed gently. "I can help you look, if you want."

"Thanks, but I've already looked everywhere. And my sister's coming soon, and I'm so not ready."

"Okay, breathe. Tell me what you need at my store, and I'll get it together while you buy groceries."

"Are you sure?"

"Yes."

I gave her the list I'd scribbled, hoping she wouldn't question why I needed more wood and nails. She quickly disappeared inside Hayden & Sons, and I continued to the grocery store without anything resembling a list. What did Chloe even like to eat? As I strolled up and down the aisles, straining my memory, I waited for something to stand out to me. My gaze landed on a box of macaroni and cheese. I was about to put it in my cart when I hesitated. Sure, she used to guzzle mac n' cheese with the best of them, but she lived in LA now. What did people in LA eat? Fancy salads? Kimchi? Street tacos?

Whatever, I thought, putting the macaroni in the cart.

Two varieties of cereal, one loaf of bread, and three packages of Oreos later, I left the store in a better mood than I'd entered it. Some things, like Chloe's love of carbs, would never change.

-------◄O►-------

THERE WERE SO MANY things I'd wanted to accomplish before
Chloe came – fixing up her bedroom, finishing the loft, attempting to bake her favorite cookies (snickerdoodles). But when I
checked my calendar, I realized that Chloe would arrive tomorrow, and those three weeks of preparation were long gone.
What I had done during them, I had no idea, and it didn't
really matter. Now there was only time to squeeze in the bare
necessities. As soon as I got home, I found my phone and texted
Chloe.

> M: What time does your flight land tomorrow?
> C: 8:04
> M: AM or PM?
> C: PM, obvs.
> M: My time or your time?
> C: Your time. I told you this already!
> M: Sorry, must've deleted the message on accident.
> C: Well, don't "accidentally" forget to pick me up
> M: Ha!
> M: What airport again?
> M: Kidding.

I hadn't been kidding, but I knew that the nearest airport was
an hour away in Manchester, and I also vaguely remembered a
conversation with Chloe about it. Great. Another big chunk cut
out of my prep time.

There was a ton to do, but first I made a cup of the tea I'd
gotten from the New Age shop. It didn't smell any better in liquid
form. Surprisingly, the taste wasn't bad. I'd never been a huge
fan of tea, but this didn't seem any worse than any other tea. And
if it actually worked, if it actually fixed my memory, I wouldn't
care if it tasted like urine.

Properly repairing the wall in Simon's room took the rest of the day. It wasn't my best work, but at least it kept the cold air out. I abandoned the idea of the loft being ready for me to sleep in. While Chloe was there, I would sleep on the couch, and I'd make it my top priority to buy a bed after she left.

Wall complete, I made myself lie down for a while, though I knew I wouldn't sleep. At four in the morning, I was up again. I drank more tea and then coffee as I organized and re-organized the kitchen cabinets. As the sun and the birds started waking up, I was arranging a few small things I'd bought for Chloe's room — an extra phone charger, a bottle of her favorite lotion, one of the packages of Oreos, and a keychain with a swan, like Cygnus. I'd ordered it for her Christmas present, and then Christmas never really happened.

Around nine, there was a knock on the door, but when I opened it, nobody was there. I walked down the front porch steps and stood in the driveway, looking left and right. I even squinted at the treeline, half-expecting to see Lester watching me. Not a soul in sight.

Then I saw the box. It was a little bigger than a shoebox, and yet I'd stepped right over without noticing it. I glanced around once more. Someone had obviously left this here. How had they disappeared so quickly?

Maybe they haven't disappeared at all.

Leaving the box, I made a quick circuit of the house, my head constantly swiveling. Lester was pretty spry for his age, but not *that* spry. And it had to have been Lester. Who else could have put Simon's box on my porch? I was certain it was Simon's box — the one he'd been buried in all those years ago — though why I was so certain I didn't know. I'd never seen it before. Or had I?

Unsuccessful, I returned to the porch, sat on the top step, and rested the box on my lap. Since Lester had said the box was empty, I expected it to be light, but it had some heft to it. I lifted the lid, then immediately dropped it again.

"Fuck, what is that?"

Covering my nose with one hand, I opened the lid with the other. Inside the box was an orange object with a tapered end and three black spots, almost like eyes and a nose. The wider end was bloody, like it had been torn off a living creature. If it hadn't been for the single white feather, I might never have guessed that I was looking at a swan's beak.

Gagging, I made to close the box, but then I saw red writing on the inside of the lid, sloppy yet in a format immediately recognizable, a poem I'd read a thousand times. This time, the words were different.

> *Simon gets inside your head*
> *Simon turns your joy to dread*
> *Simon seeks a lonely host*
> *Simon takes who you love most*

CHAPTER 20

THE POEM REVERBERATED IN my head the whole drive to the airport. The last line in particular wouldn't leave me alone:

Simon takes who you love most

Chloe. Everything pointed to Chloe – not just the poem, but the swan beak and feather. Cygnus. Chloe.

"You don't even know if that was real," I told myself, smacking the steering wheel. "If that really happened, where is the box? Where is the swan beak? It was just a messed-up dream."

But what did it mean Simon would "take" her? Even if he was a freaky bird ghost, he was still just a bird, and a fairly small one at that. It couldn't be a literal taking.

"What have you done with them? Where are my children? Now he's got all your souls."

The words popped into my head, accompanied by an image of a woman dragging three screaming children through the trees. It played almost like a movie, yet I knew it wasn't from any movie I'd seen. The woman's name was on the tip of my tongue, and the little girls were Sharon and Sylvia, and the boy was...

A sudden, aggressive honk made my head snap up, and my hands jerked the wheel. To my left, the driver of the sedan I'd almost hit flipped me off as he zoomed past.

"Sorry," I said, wincing.

Try as I might to shake the feeling that something was off, I couldn't, and the closer I got to the airport, the stronger the feeling got. When I saw the blonde girl leaning against a pillar outside baggage claim, typing on her phone, unease blossomed into full-blown dread. What would I see when she lifted her head? Would it be the real Chloe, or would it be almost her but not quite?

She spotted my truck, and her face lit up. Her only luggage was a backpack, which she slung over one shoulder before hurrying to meet me. Briefly, my dread lifted. It was Chloe. Only Chloe. Pink-cheeked and grinning and still my baby sister. Right?

"Eeeee," Chloe squealed, sliding into the passenger seat and throwing her arms around me. "Oh my god, I missed you!"

"I missed you too," I said, hugging her back.

"Wow, you've really embraced the whole outdoorsy culture."

"What do you mean?"

She tugged playfully on my forest-green fleece pullover. "It's cute."

"It's warm," I said, pulling away from the curb. "Speaking of which, you're going to freeze in that." I nodded at her ripped black jeans and stylishly baggy black sweater. "Didn't I tell you to pack warm clothes?"

"This is the warmest I have." She shrugged. "I'm from LA, not the Arctic."

"Lucky for you, the Arctic has some extra clothes."

"Is there an extra one of those pullovers?"

"Shut up," I said, grinning.

Why had I been so worried? Chloe was her usual sassy self, and our rapport was totally normal. During the drive home, we discussed plans for that week, and I had to remind her yet again that there wasn't a nightlife scene in Arden Woods or any other town nearby. She oohed and ahhed over the moonlit mountain views and asked nervously if she should be worried about the signs warning of falling rocks.

I kept shooting glances at her as though expecting her to disappear. After the fourth time I did this, she asked, "Why are you looking at me like that?"

"Can't believe you're here, I guess. Part of me thought you'd bail like at Thanksgiving."

Chloe grimaced. "Yeah. About that. It was really sucky of me, and I'm sorry."

"Why did you do it?"

"Because I still hated LA, and I genuinely thought if I came home, I'd never leave again."

"Would that have been so bad?"

"Yes. No? I don't know." Chloe shrugged. "But I had it all wrong. When I went home for Christmas, it was great, and I feel like it kind of gave me the strength to go back and to really start making LA my home."

She went home, realized it wasn't home anymore, and wasn't afraid to leave. Spending time with family had just reinforced her decision to move away from them. Would the same happen after her visit with me?

"I can't wait to see Monster," Chloe said, changing the subject. "Is he with a friend, or did you leave him at the house?"

Her expression grew more somber with each word as I explained about Monster running away.

"That's what I want to do this week," she declared when I was done. "Find Monster."

"But he could be anywhere by now, and I checked everywhere nearby."

"Doesn't matter, I still want to look. And it'll give you a chance to try to turn me into a New Englander."

When we pulled up to the house, Chloe seemed in genuine awe.

"It looks so good!" she said, hopping out and moving closer. "Like, brand new."

"Chloe, it's dark outside. You can hardly see it."

"I can see enough."

"You don't even know what it looked like before."

"Yeah, but you told me it was shit, and this is beautiful. Very rustic."

"Rustic in a good way? Or rustic in an 'I'm-just-being-polite' kind of way?"

"Have I ever tried to be polite to you?"

"Good point. Let's go in."

I gave her the grand tour, even showing her the unfinished loft.

"It doesn't look like much now," I said quickly. "But I want to turn it into a bedroom-slash-library."

"Paint me a word-picture."

As I described and gestured, I could see the wheels in her head turning. She gave several suggestions and statements that all centered around trends she'd seen in LA. By the time we were done with the inside tour, I was already sick of hearing about LA. I understood she'd been absorbing her new culture, but every time she said "LA", it was a barb in my heart.

"We should go shopping one day this week," Chloe proclaimed, settling on the couch and mussing her hair, which was starting to grow darker blonde roots.

"For?"

"House stuff. I already Googled it. There's a home goods store only half an hour away, and there's this cute little diner near it."

"That sounds fun," I said, a little irritated that she was making plans on my turf.

"Cool. What else are we doing while I'm here?"

"Um..."

It hadn't occurred to me that Chloe might expect 24/7 entertainment. There wasn't much to be had out here, especially after 9 PM.

"We could go into town tomorrow," I suggested. "Get coffee at Beans & Brews. And you could meet my friend Hannah."

"Nah." Chloe draped her legs over my lap. "I'm not ready to share you yet."

"Okay," I said, secretly pleased. "I could show you the prop-erty. It's got some interesting features."

"Ugh, you sound just like Kim."

"Kim?"

"Our cousin, Kim. The realtor. Remember two Christmases ago when she 'just stopped by' with all those cookies because she got the slightest whiff that Mom and Dad might possibly be thinking about selling their house?"

Not at all. "Yeah, sure. She'd hate it up here. All the houses are so old and need tons of work."

Chloe gave me a strange look. "She's already up here, re-member? She and Grayson moved to Vermont?"

"Oh, did they?"

"Yeah, Dad was worried about Grayson moving to a new environment after the problems he's had in school. He says they're doing pretty well, though. You should go visit them sometime."

So, Grayson was a child, not her husband. That seemed like a bit of knowledge I should definitely possess, and yet I was struggling to even remember Kim – what she looked like, whether we had played together as kids, why she was a single mom. Whether she came from my dad's side or my mom's side. There was a big blank in my mind where Kim should've been.

"Can we go look for Monster?" Chloe asked.

"It's pitch-black out there."

"So? You have flashlights, right? I can't rest until I at least try to find my favorite nephew."

"Your favorite nephew? What about Aiden?"

"I said what I said."

"You'll need to bundle up before we go out," I said, sliding out from under Chloe's legs and standing. "I'm sure it's below freezing."

I lent her long underwear to go under her ripped jeans, thick socks, a fleece pullover, and a knit hat. She still swore loudly at how cold it was outside. I was about ready to tell her I'd changed

my mind and we should go back in when she started calling
Monster.

"Here, boy!" She whistled and patted her thighs. "Come here,
Monster!"

We walked down past the fireplace and the well, all the
way beyond Lester's house. I had told her a bit about him, so
she peered curiously through the frosty trees, but Lester was
nowhere in sight.

"Maybe he has Monster," Chloe said as we turned and headed
back.

"What?"

"Maybe Lester took him."

"Why would he do that?"

She shrugged. "Monster's a desirable breed. Lots of people
want them."

"Not Lester. He's terrified of him."

"He may act that way, but hasn't he done some sketchy stuff
before?"

"I don't know."

"Didn't you say he broke into your house?"

"I thought he did, but it wasn't him. It wasn't anybody. I just
misplaced a few things."

"Oh. Still, it might not hurt to pay Lester a visit, right?"

"Maybe."

As we trekked back past my house, I scanned the waterline
with my flashlight as I'd done many times since Monster's disap-
pearance. My greatest fear was that I would find him there, dead
and frozen, with stiff fur and ice-crusted eyes. But he wasn't
there. He wasn't on the other side of the property, either. The
only unusual thing that happened was Chloe's foot slipping into
the hole beside the boulder. Yelping, she slid and landed on her
backside.

"I told you to bring good boots," I said, helping her up.

"Well, even good boots can't stop you from falling in a hole,"
she said grumpily.

"That's so weird. I thought I covered it up so Monster wouldn't get into it." I knelt, peering into the hole. "I'm nearly positive I put my toolbox over the hole."

"Lester must've taken that, too."

———— ◆ ————

THE NEXT THREE DAYS of the visit passed without anything of much interest or excitement. We shopped, decorated, and ate at restaurants. We got coffee, and I introduced Chloe to Hannah, and they seemed to get along well. We took long walks and had lots of fires in the pit outside and made s'mores. We looked (unsuccessfully) for Monster.

Then, on the fourth night, I brought home Thai food from the restaurant in Arden Woods.

"It's really good," I assured Chloe as I unpacked the bags. "And I got yours with zero spice, I promise."

"If I lose my tastebuds over this, I'm blaming you."

"Fair enough. Remember the one Thai place near home? With the worst spring rolls of all time?"

She frowned. "I don't remember a Thai place."

"It was where the Mexican restaurant used to be, and all the Thai food kind of tasted like refried beans."

Chloe shook her head, brow furrowed.

"Maybe you never went," I said. "Daniel dragged me there a few times."

"You mean the Mexican restaurant on Shaw Street?"

"Yep."

"It's still there. Or at least it was before I left for LA."

"Huh. It must've changed back. I'm not surprised that Thai place didn't last."

"I wonder what the best Thai food in LA is. Alice will know."

"Who's Alice?"

"Fabi's girlfriend. I'm pretty sure she's half Thai. She and Johnny both. At least, that's what Rae told me."

Not a single one of those names meant anything to me. There had been a time – not that long ago – when Chloe and I knew all the same people. Neighbors, old teachers, people from our parents' church, people we'd gone to school with. Now she was spewing names at random, or at least that was how it seemed to me.

"You sure have a lot of new friends," I said, filling two glasses with iced water. "New friends every time I talk to you."

"So?" she said, sounding defensive. "That's what you're supposed to do when you move to a new place. Just because you've only made one friend since you got here..."

"I'm not being accusatory. It's just that I've never heard you say any of those names before."

"You have; you just didn't bother to remember."

"Okay, okay. Chill."

I arranged all the food on the table, grabbed utensils and napkins from the kitchen, and finally took my seat. My mouth watered at the aroma of yellow curry. Prying off the lid, I took a couple of warm, flavorful bites before realizing that Chloe hadn't touched her Pad Thai.

"What's wrong?" I asked. "Too spicy?"

"There's peanuts on it."

"Of course there are peanuts."

"You didn't ask them to remove them?"

"Why would I? That's part of Pad Thai."

"I'm allergic."

I smiled skeptically. Was this some new LA thing? "Since when?"

"Since always."

"Then why haven't I heard of it before?"

"You have." Chloe's voice was rising. "It's been a huge deal my entire life. I've been to the hospital, like, five times. You even drove me there once. Remember? You'd just turned sixteen, and you didn't have your license yet, but Mom and Dad and Andy were out of town, so you had to take me to the ER?"

It sounded like a made-up story from a TV drama, not something I had lived through. Was she pulling my leg? She didn't sound like she was joking. Chloe must've seen the doubt on my face, because she grunted in frustration and pushed her chair back from the table.

"My hands are itching just from being close to them," she said, taking several steps away from the table and crossing her arms over her chest.

"That seems a little extreme."

"Well, it's an *extreme* allergy."

I wanted to believe her, but I didn't. I'd been losing patches of memories, sure, but this allergy – if it existed – was way too big to forget. Hadn't I made peanut butter cookies at home a dozen times? And hadn't I made her PB&Js for lunch when she was little? A whole slew of my memories contradicted her, and I had to trust in the memories I retained.

"Do you seriously think I'm lying?" Chloe demanded. "Or being dramatic?"

I opened my mouth to respond, but no words came out.

For a second, I saw it in her face.

That flash of nonrecognition.

No. Please, not Chloe. Please, Simon, don't take her, don't turn her into an imposter.

"Why are you looking at me like that?"

"Never mind," I said, swallowing hard and staring at the ground. "Chloe, you're my sister, right? And you'll always be my sister?"

A pause. Too long. Too, too long.

"Of course," she said. "Even if you did try to kill me."

"I didn't – I didn't mean to. I just forgot."

But if I could forget a lethal allergy, what else would I forget about her? How long until her face became a stranger's? In order to keep her, I would have to keep her at a distance.

"I think you should leave early," I said, finally looking up at her. "Tomorrow."

She stopped scratching her palm. "What?"

"I need you to leave."

"What the hell, Michelle. My flight isn't until Friday."

"Then go online and change it. I'll pay."

Angry tears filled her eyes. "Why are you being like this?"

"Because I have no idea who you are anymore. All you talk about is LA, and places I've never seen, and people I've never met. You've got a new life out there, and that's fine, but our worlds don't match up anymore. Let's be real."

"Let's be real?" she scoffed. "You *really* need help. Mom and Dad think you're an alcoholic. They practically begged me to come up here and check on you since you haven't called them in weeks."

"I'm not an alcoholic."

"Yeah, I know. I checked everywhere and didn't find so much as a bottle of vanilla extract."

"So, you only came to spy on me for Mom and Dad."

"No, I came because I missed you." She took a step closer to me. "I understand why you never told me. You know, about the alcohol thing. But I wish you had."

"I was protecting you."

"I'm your sister. You don't need to protect me. Not from you."

Chloe reached for my arm, and I flinched, afraid that if she touched me, it would make everything worse. She pulled her hand back, shoved it in her pocket, and strode into the guest bedroom. A minute later, she emerged dressed in the winter clothes I'd loaned her, marched straight past me, and went out the back door. To my relief, she turned right toward Lester's house rather than left toward the hole.

CHAPTER 21

CHLOE DIDN'T RETURN UNTIL nearly midnight. I was waiting for her, sitting at the table with a cup of ginkgo biloba tea, not knowing what on earth to say, but she ignored me and went straight to her room. Knowing she must be starving, I made mac and cheese and set a bowl of it outside her door before retreating to the loft. In spite of everything, I smiled to myself when I heard her door open and shut again, followed by the clink of a fork.

What she didn't understand was that I was doing both of us a favor. If she stayed here, even for another day, Simon would take her. He would steal her soul and replace her with an imposter, like he had with the Dennis children. She would no longer be herself, and I would no longer know her.

Simon gets inside your head
Simon turns your joy to dread
Simon seeks a lonely host
Simon takes who you love most

For whatever reason, Simon had latched onto me. He wanted to hurt me, and the best way to do that was by taking Chloe away from me.

After a long, sleepless night, I went downstairs to scramble some eggs only to find Chloe standing at the front door, fully dressed, backpack on her shoulders. Her gaze remained on the floor. The shadows under her eyes told me that she hadn't slept either.

"My flight leaves at noon," she said. "We should go ahead and go."

"Do you want any breakfast?"

"No."

The temperature had plummeted overnight, and it took a while to defrost the truck's windshield.

Note to self: finish the garage so I can keep my truck inside.

Chloe waited in the passenger seat while I scraped ice off the windows. In the corner of my eye, the dark, dragon-like shape of Simon lurked in a nearby pine tree. He was watching. He was waiting. But I wasn't going to let him take my sister. Working faster, I cleared the windows, and then we were off.

It was a silent drive. Beside me, Chloe typed away on her phone, probably texting a roommate asking if they could pick her up from the airport. Or maybe she was texting our parents, giving them a full report of my erratic behavior. My throat tightened.

When we finally arrived at the airport after what felt like ten hours, I pulled up to the curb and parked, not knowing what to expect next. Would she hug me? Would she even say goodbye?

"I'm sorry if I..." I started, then trailed off, not sure where to go next. "I'm sorry if it feels like I kicked you out."

"If? It definitely feels like that."

"I've loved having you here. It's just... there are things you don't understand."

Things I'm not even sure I understand.

"Then help me understand."

Chloe turned to me, trying to meet my gaze, but I kept my eyes on my lap. If I told her about Simon or about the things I'd seen in that house or even about the big black holes in my memory, she'd think I was crazy. She'd tell my parents, and they'd try to send me to rehab that I didn't need.

"You should get going," I said. "Might take a while to get through security."

"Yeah," she said, deflated. "Sure."

She opened the door and slid out onto the pavement, holding her backpack but not putting it on yet. I got that flash again, like I was looking at a stranger. If she didn't leave soon, I'd lose her forever.

"This is for you," she said, holding out an envelope. "It's your birthday present. I forgot to give it to you earlier."

Inside the envelope was a sheet of temporary tattoos, all of them swans.

"I know it's not much, but it made me think of you and of last summer."

"Thanks," I said lamely, still not looking her in the eye. "Have a safe trip. Text me when you make it back."

She gave a half-hearted wave, shouldered her backpack, and disappeared inside. I watched her all the way up the escalator to the security checkpoint. She didn't look back once.

⸻◆⸻

"SHE'S ADJUSTING SO MUCH better than I am," I told Hannah later that afternoon when I stopped by her store. "She's making so many friends that I can't keep up with them. And she seems so at home there already."

"You say it like it's a bad thing," said Hannah, frowning slightly.

"Maybe it is. She doesn't even seem like herself anymore."

"Hm."

"You think I'm overreacting."

"I'm not an expert at migrating. Or sisters, for that matter. But sometimes, you kind of have to become a different person to adapt to a new situation, don't you?"

"I'm not any different, though. I'm still me. I don't suddenly have a whole new life and a whole new circle of people."

"You kind of do. I mean, think about your life a year ago versus now."

She had a point. A year ago, I'd been married and working as an architect in Indiana, hanging out with the same people I'd hung out with my entire life, eating the same pizza every single Friday night. Now, I'd renovated almost an entire house, I was living on my own, which I'd never done before, and the only old friend I saw regularly was Spencer, at least before our fight.

"Do you want some lotion?"

"Huh?" I asked, snapping out of my daze.

"Lotion? For your arm?"

I realized I'd been scratching my left arm, leaving red streaks from my elbow to my wrist. I pulled my hand away and my sleeve down, not wanting her to see the few scars that remained from when I'd scratched myself bloody at Thanksgiving. "No, that's okay. It's just a nervous tic."

"You need to watch out for dry skin, though. It can be an issue up here."

"I bought some good lotion, I'm just not sure where it is."

"You really misplace things a lot, don't you?"

"Recently, yes. Speaking of which, I need another box of nails."

"Seriously?" She grinned, half-amused and half-exasperated. "I've already had to up my stock for you."

"Sorry," I said, wincing apologetically.

We talked a bit more, and I paid for the nails. As I was leaving, she asked, "Any update on Monster?"

"Who?"

"Monster," she enunciated, thinking I hadn't heard her.

I paused – just a beat, yet long enough – and said, "Oh. Nothing yet. Still looking."

My legs shook so badly that I almost didn't make it to the truck. *Why did I have to think about who Monster was? Why had I paused?* Now that I'd pushed Chloe out, Monster was the only tether I had left, the only familiar piece of my life. I couldn't lose him. I had to keep looking, and I had to remember.

"Fuck you, Simon," I muttered. "You can't have him either."

———— ◆○◆ ————

THAT WHOLE AFTERNOON AND evening, I searched once more for Monster. The cold was so intense that it permeated all my layers of clothing; my toes and nose went numb, but I kept looking. And when there was nowhere else to look, I turned to the well, the one I'd sworn to always leave shut. As far as I could remember, I hadn't removed the stone cover once. Even if the cover had been off, though, Monster wouldn't have jumped inside. All the same, I felt compelled to look.

Small flakes of snow dusted my shoulders as I stood by the well. For a moment, I could've sworn I heard a faint voice, though I couldn't make out its words. Bracing myself against the heavy stone cover, I pushed. After several grunting heaves, it slid off, landing with a crash and cracking in two.

Holding my breath, I peered over the edge. The well was deeper than I'd expected, and I couldn't see the bottom. My hand trembled as I held out my phone, hoping the light would reveal no fur or floppy ears, nothing but the shimmer of water far below. Then the phone slipped from my fingers. The light swung crazily as it plummeted, and I caught glimpses of mossy stones and what might have been the remnant of an old rope. Finally, the phone landed with a crunch that told me the screen had cracked. The flashlight still worked, though, and my flesh turned clammy when I saw what it illuminated.

A full skeleton, scraps of clothes clinging to it, sitting up and leaning against the side of the well.

"Kent," I breathed. "It has to be him."

If you find them in the hole, that's not really them, they're imposters, Shirley had written.

Kent had been in a hole, too, it turned out.

I leaned farther into the well, squinting at the clothing. Lester had mentioned that Kent was wearing his favorite orange shirt when he disappeared, and indeed the shreds of cloth were a faded orange.

There was something else down there, too. To get a better look, I stood on tiptoe, leaning far out over the well. A sudden rush of wings behind me made me jump, and I overbalanced, tipping forward. My hands scraped the sides of the well, turning bloody and raw as I tried to slow my descent. At the last second, I wrapped my arms around my head.

The impact rattled my bones, but nothing appeared to be broken. In a panic, I tried to climb out, but my boots slipped on the moss, and my fingernails tore on the rough stones. Giving up, I sat across from Kent's skeleton and hugged my knees to my chest.

"Your dad's been looking for you," I told him. "Maybe I'll take you home."

His skull drooped onto his shoulder, almost like he was considering my offer. But I had no idea how to get myself, let alone Kent's skeleton, out of the well. The walls were too slick to climb. My smashed phone had no reception. And when I looked up, I was horrified to see that someone had put the stone cover back on. There was no gray-white snowy sky. Only darkness.

A scream burgeoned inside me. As it released, I woke up, sweating and shaking. I was on the couch, and the phone clutched in my hand was perfectly intact. In fact, its buzz had pulled me out of that terrible dream.

C: Made it home

I typed a response and deleted it. Lying back down, I stared at the ceiling, waiting for my heart to slow. My head and hands throbbed like I really had fallen in the well.

And they were itchy. So itchy.

THE NEXT MORNING, AS I brushed my hair, I noticed that there was new growth on the bald spots. *Good, but now I wish my fucking skin would stop itching so badly.* I braided my hair tightly to keep it out of the way. Then I drank coffee, ate scrambled eggs on toast, and went to tackle the garage.

Much as I needed a place to keep my truck, I hadn't set foot in the garage since the forensics team's final visit. Part of me was afraid of finding more bones, even though the police had been very thorough. But with at least another month of heavy winter ahead, I was done delaying.

It was time to make this place my home. No more excuses.

The garage was a mess of broken concrete, shards of wood, and fingerprint dust. There was no point in trying to recover the wooden structure, as it had rotted in several places, so I knocked down what remained of the walls and threw the wooden beams in a heap in the yard. Then, it was time to remove the old foundation. Before long, I was coated in white powder even thicker than the falling snow. It took most of the day to break up the rest of the concrete and haul the slabs out of the way.

Thankfully, there was no more precipitation in the forecast for ten days, which would give me time to pour a new foundation and let it set. I had never poured a foundation before, but the idea was very appealing. A new foundation for the garage to match the new foundation for me.

When the sun dipped below the trees, I turned to go back inside and clean up. I had barely taken two steps when I spotted movement in the forest. The hair on the back of my neck stood up, and I froze. Though the woods were already dim with dusk, I saw a flash of dark fur and big paws.

Holy fuck, it's a wolf!

I bolted across the yard and inside, slamming the door behind me. A moment later, something scratched at the door, asking to be let in. Trembling, I peered out the side window and spotted an enormous beast on my porch, sitting there calm as anything. As I watched, it pawed at the door again.

I fumbled for my phone and searched for the animal control number.

"Lancaster County Animal Control."

"Are there wolves around here? I'm pretty sure there's a wolf outside. Fuck, it's huge."

"What's your address?"

"214 New Hampshire Route, uh, 58."

A long pause. "Ma'am, are you sure it isn't a coyote?"

"So what if it is? It's got to weigh a hundred and fifty pounds, and it won't leave my porch."

"Stay inside, and we'll send someone your way. They should arrive in half an hour."

"Half an hour?" I protested, but the man had already hung up.

Looking through the window again, I saw that the beast was now walking along the side of the house, sniffing at all the doors and windows, whining softly.

When it went around to the deck, I ducked into the downstairs bedroom to stay out of sight. Waiting for animal control to arrive, I sat on the edge of the bed, tapping my dirty boot against the floor, shedding concrete dust on the comforter. Unable to stay still, I paced the room, distracting myself by planning out the next steps for the garage.

First, I would need to lay out the rebar and slabs to mark the outline of the foundation, then lay the foundation itself. It was only a rectangle – how difficult could it be? After the foundation set, I'd need to construct the garage itself. I would definitely need more timber, but I wasn't certain about the nails. It seemed like I had bought some recently, but where were they?

Vaguely, I remembered storing the nails in the utility closet across the hall. It was right beside the guest bathroom, and I'd only been in there a handful of times. It was long, narrow, dark, and dirty, and I wondered why I hadn't done any work on it yet. I must've forgotten it existed.

"If I were a box of nails," I mused, perusing the nearly bare, dusty shelves, "where would I be?"

Though I searched extensively, I couldn't find them. Convinced that I would need to return to Hayden & Sons to buy a new box, I turned to leave, but then I spotted a cabinet I'd missed before.

"Okay, nails, you have to be in there," I commanded, placing my fingers on the handles.

I pulled open the cabinet.

It was stacked, top to bottom, with boxes and boxes of nails.

❈

FOR FAR TOO LONG, I stared at the cabinet of nails. Just how many boxes had I bought? One by one, I pulled them out, counting thirty-one in total.

"I need another box of nails."

"I must have misplaced it."

"I used more than expected."

All those nails had been in this cabinet the whole time.

There wasn't time to think about it, though, because I heard the crunch of gravel as a car pulled into my driveway. But it wasn't animal control — it was Hannah.

When I saw her car, my pulse accelerated. I looked everywhere for the wolf but couldn't find it. Then I stood in the front window, waving, hoping Hannah would see me and get the message to stay in her car. Instead, to my surprise and horror, she walked right up to the wolf, which had reappeared suddenly, drawn by the noise of her car.

"Wait," I cried, stepping onto my front porch. "Stay away!"

Hannah looked around in confusion. She was so close to the wolf that it made my heart thrum painfully, yet she didn't seem panicked or afraid.

"Get away from it!" I shouted.

A van pulled into the driveway. On its side, in huge green letters, were the words "Lancaster County Animal Control". A man and a woman got out, and I immediately jumped down the steps and waved them down, jabbing a finger toward the beast.

"That's it," I yelled. "That's the wolf!"

The two of them and Hannah stared at me for so long.

"Well?" I demanded. "Are you going to help, or are you going to let it attack my friend?"

The man snorted, as if I'd told a mildly amusing joke. Then he seemed to realize I was serious. He cleared his throat.

"Ma'am, your friend is fine. That isn't a wolf; it's a Bernese mountain dog. A very gentle one, too. See?"

Looking closer, I saw that he was right. The dog was indeed enormous and shaggy, the coloring on its face obscured by dirt, but its tail was wagging as Hannah scratched its ears. Sighing with relief, I took a few steps toward them. The dog let out a yip and cowered against Hannah's legs.

"What's wrong with him?" she asked.

"He looks like he's been living rough for a while," I said, examining the twigs and matted clumps in the dog's long fur.

"A few weeks, right? Didn't you say he ran away right after New Year's?"

"Hang on," said the woman from animal control, who was still standing beside the van. "Are you telling me that she called us about her own dog?"

Hannah's gaze moved from me to the woman and back again, connecting the dots.

"You called animal control?" she asked in disbelief.

"I saw a large beast roaming my property, and it scared me, so yes, I called animal control," I said defensively, not sure why she was acting affronted.

"You guys can go," said Hannah to the animal control workers. "I know this dog. I'll take care of it."

Once they were gone, Hannah coaxed the dog into the back of her car and shut the door gently. Then she rounded on me, boots crunching on the gravel, eyes alight with a fury I'd never seen before.

"What's wrong with you?" she demanded.

"Um..." *Where to begin?*

"Why are you acting like you've never seen Monster before?"

"I guess I didn't recognize him."

In truth, I still didn't. If I owned a dog, why wasn't there a dog bed or food in my house? And if Monster was mine, why had he shied away from me like I frightened him?

"You didn't recognize the dog you've had for two years," scoffed Hannah. "The dog you brought to my store all the time, the dog you ended your friendship with Spencer over."

"I didn't end my friendship with Spencer; we're just in a fight."

"Yeah, a fight that's lasted weeks."

"What are you doing here, anyway?"

"Are you serious? You invited me."

"I did?"

Pulling her phone out, she opened up her messages and held it out for me to read. The texts were from this morning.

M: Hey, know anything about foundations?
H: Are we talking makeup or concrete?
M: LOL
M: Concrete, definitely.
H: Thank god
H: Yeah, actually I've helped lay a few house foundations. Are you building something new?

M: Redoing the garage and need some advice. Are you free this afternoon?

H: Sure, what time?

M: Maybe 6?

The time on the phone was 6:13 PM. I looked up at Hannah, and she must've seen in my eyes that I had no memory of sending those messages, no memory of our arrangements.

"Okay," said Hannah evenly, slipping the phone back into her coat pocket. "Okay. You're obviously going through some shit right now, so I'll take care of Monster for a while, okay?"

"Yeah, okay."

"Before I go, is there anything I can do for you? Anyone I can call?"

"Oh, thanks, but I'm fine. Really."

"Well, when you decide you want Monster back..."

She trailed off, shrugging. Then she got in the car and drove away, the dog peering at me through the back windshield with mournful brown eyes.

CHAPTER 22

FOR THE FIRST TIME in weeks, Spencer called me. Momentarily ignoring that I was furious at him for some reason I couldn't recall, I answered.

"My cousin Dana is going to take a look at you," he said without preamble. "Don't worry, she won't charge anything. Can you be at my house at noon?"

"I told you; I don't need to see a doctor. There's no point, because I know what they'll say."

"You do?"

Damn it. "I mean, I know it can't be anything good," I said quickly.

"All the more reason to go. Don't be that person who never gets checked out and then suddenly is dying of cancer because they were too stupid and stubborn for it to be caught early."

"I'm guessing you talked to Hannah about yesterday?"

"I did, but stop trying to deflect me." Spencer cleared his throat. "I'm just looking out for you, Michelle. That's what friends do."

The tears on my cheeks, thin and cold, startled me. Yesterday evening, as Hannah's taillights had disappeared, I'd had to face the fact that I might have just alienated the one person here I still considered to be a friend, all over a dog that I didn't remember owning. In spite of the photos on my phone showing me posing with a Bernese mountain dog, I had trouble connecting it to the dog I'd seen prowling my yard. Memories lurked beneath the surface, murky and jumbled.

But Hannah was still my friend, and so was Spencer, and they were right. I needed help.

"Noon?" I asked finally, shakily.

"Yeah. And no matter what happens, I'm here for you. Just like that time you did three shots of absinthe and vomited all over my car."

I choked out a wet laugh, said goodbye, and hung up.

With a couple of hours to spare and my mood spiraling, a walk was necessary. Pulling on fleece-lined leggings, a long-sleeved shirt, my thick plaid jacket, and boots, I went out the front door. As I turned to lock it, I caught movement in the glass and spun around. A dark shape perched in the lower branches of a white pine tree.

"It's not him," I said, tapping a fist against the side of my head. "It's not Simon. Simon is dead."

Simon fluttered from the tree to the cab of my truck, staring at me the whole time with his dark, sunken eyes.

"No," I said, stepping forward and waving my arms. "Shoo!"

Simon's dragonesque head cocked to the side. He flew at me.

Raising my arms to protect my face, I stumbled down the steps and across the gravel to the truck and climbed inside, fending off Simon's beating wings and tearing claws. Somehow, I managed to close the truck door, though Simon still came at it, talons screeching across glass and metal.

Without thinking, I cranked the engine, and the truck roared to life. Throwing it into gear, I hurtled down the driveway at breakneck speed and swerved out onto the thankfully empty road. It took me a few seconds to realize that Simon hadn't followed me. Not wanting to go back yet, I kept driving toward Arden Woods. My heart pounded the whole way there, and my hands gripped the steering wheel so hard that my palms burned and my knuckles turned white.

Things had gotten so bad. Simon's attacks weren't just psychological anymore. Hannah and Spencer were right that I needed help, but maybe they were wrong about the type of help. A nurse could decipher my symptoms and maybe alleviate them. They couldn't help with Simon, though.

Mystic Crystals, the New Age shop in Arden Woods, was exactly what I expected it to be. The shop was small, creaky, and crammed with shelves, every surface occupied. There were pewter figurines of fairies and dragons, plastic bins of brightly-colored gemstones, and candles in every size, color, and scent. The air was filled with a confusing mixture of smells from the candles and the packets of incense.

The woman behind the counter didn't immediately look up when I entered. In direct opposition to the shop, *she* was not at all what I had expected. In fact, her appearance was almost a parody of normalcy. She wore unflattering mom jeans, a purple sweatshirt, and white tennis shoes. Her iron-gray hair was in a typical short, old-lady haircut, and reading glasses hung on a delicate silver chain around her neck.

"Hello?" I said, and the word came out as a trembling whisper.

The woman looked up, peering over her glasses, and I could immediately tell from her expression that this wasn't the first time she'd seen me.

"I've been here before, haven't I?" I said.

"Twice," said the woman, folding up her glasses and letting them dangle from the chain. "Obviously, that ginkgo biloba tea didn't do a thing."

I stared at her blankly, not remembering any tea, and as I stared, something in her face started to look familiar. If she was right and I'd been here twice already, that might explain it. But that wasn't it. I'd seen her somewhere before, recently.

"Come here, sweetie," said the woman, beckoning me closer.

She came out from behind the counter and put an arm around my shoulders, patting me comfortingly.

"Is there anyone I can call for you?"

Her words echoed what Hannah had said the other day, and thinking of Hannah made me think of her grandfather and how reluctant he'd been to talk about the Dennis family, and then I thought of the fact that Sylvia Dennis had lived in my house and had a breakdown there, like I was apparently having now.

And then I remembered the picture of Sylvia at the Waterside Children's Home, her olive-green eyes and distinctive bowed lips and freckles.

"You're...Sylvia Dennis, aren't you?"

The woman immediately pulled her arm away, her expression flicking from kind concern to cold guardedness.

"You are, aren't you." It was no longer a question.

After a moment's calculation, the woman said, "And you're the damn fool who bought that house."

She turned and marched toward the back of the shop, and I followed, nearly tripping over my own feet. When Sylvia pushed through a beaded curtain, I did the same and found myself in a storage/break room. Coffee brewed on a chipped countertop, and metal shelves were stacked with boxes labeled "patchouli incense" and "soy wax".

"I've been looking everywhere for you," I said. "I tracked you as far as a mental facility in Manchester, but I couldn't figure out where you went after that."

"That's because I changed my name," Sylvia said, scowling at me. "I didn't *want* anybody to find me. You can go now, by the way."

"I thought you wanted to help me."

"I did, when I thought you only needed a ride or a cup of tea. But I'm not going to talk about that damn house or anything that happened in it."

"You keep saying 'that damn house', so does that mean you believe it's haunted?"

Sylvia's eyes narrowed. "I've done my best to bury my past, and I don't appreciate you stabbing a shovel into it. I'll ask you nicely one more time to leave."

"Please, Sylvia, I—"

"It's Susannah now."

"Okay, well, please, Susannah. I'm going crazy in that house. I have a million boxes of nails, and I thought I didn't have any, and I'm forgetting things and losing things and seeing things—"

"What things?" Sylvia interrupted again.

"Children, and, and a skeleton and feathers. And most of all, Simon, the bird."

"Simon the bird died decades ago."

"Then how is he always in the trees outside my house? And how is he..."

I trailed off, tears streaming down my face. I had suddenly remembered Monster, and the scratches on his snout, and how I hadn't even recognized him the day I called animal control, and I remembered the look on Chloe's face when I told her she had to leave.

"How is he taking everyone I love?" I asked, wiping my eyes and nose with my sleeve.

Sylvia's expression softened ever so slightly. She sighed and rubbed the bridge of her nose, and I noticed how small and delicate her hands were – the same hands that had placed Simon's box at the base of the tree, the same hands that had tried to pry her mother's fingers loose as she dragged her toward the hole under the rock.

Finally, she looked at me and said, "You'd better come with me."

———◆———

THE INSIDE OF SYLVIA'S house was as normal as she was, but in a staged kind of way. It was like she had done an internet search for "normal suburban home" and done her best to make it a reality. The entryway was decorated with professional photos of her family – a handsome, gray-haired husband; two smiling daughters; a handful of grandchildren; and a golden retriever with a bright red collar.

Sylvia led me down the hall, and I peeked into the living room, where a well-worn sofa faced a decent-sized TV, and the mantel was laden with even more family photos. On the piano in the corner, a piece of sheet music rested on the stand, as if someone had just been practicing. Everything was as tidy and homey as a house in a magazine.

"In here," said Sylvia, gesturing ahead into a light-dappled kitchen.

Snapshots and children's drawings were held to the fridge by bright, cheery magnets from local businesses. One of the drawings showed a little girl surrounded by a veritable zoo, including a dark bird. I shuddered and turned away from the fridge to face Sylvia, who was staring out the sliding glass door at a perfectly groomed back lawn.

"I brought you here so you could see what my life is like now," she said, her gaze still on the yard. "It's quiet. It's normal. It's simple and beautiful. What happened back then has no place here."

"I understand," I said, and I thought I truly did.

Her childhood had been so turbulent and traumatic that she'd made it her goal to have the mundane life she'd missed out on for years. These photographs were her way of fighting off the darkness.

"My family doesn't know anything about my past," Sylvia continued. "Not even my husband. And I'd like to keep it that way."

"Um, of course," I said, because she was looking at me expectantly. "I won't say anything."

"When I turned 18, I inherited all my parents' money, because I was the only one left to inherit it. I left the children's home and moved straight back to the house. Even now, I couldn't tell you exactly why. Maybe because it was the last place I'd been happy, the last place Simon and Sharon were alive."

A mental image came to me of the police pulling the children's frozen, starved bodies out of the hole, and I shivered.

"Obviously, I wasn't in a good state. I'd lost everybody I loved, and I wanted to see if I could get them back or at least talk to them."

"Like with a Ouija board?"

"That and any other occult shit I could get my hands on. I went pretty deep, and it got dark. When none of it worked, I tried to forget my disappointment in alcohol and drugs."

Like me, only I never had a good reason for it.

"Did you see things?" I asked. "While you lived in the house?"

"All kinds of things. A lot of the same things you said you saw. Feathers, bones, that bird, and sometimes, my family. Even... even my mother."

As she said this, Sylvia glanced at one of the photos on the fridge. She was in the middle, with a daughter on each side, and both of them strongly resembled her. Among all the dozens of pictures I'd spotted, there were none of her siblings. Maybe she just didn't have a good photo of them; or maybe part of burying her past had been forgetting about them.

"So, the house *is* haunted," I said, relieved at the confirmation. "Evil."

"Of course it isn't," Sylvia snapped, her sharp gaze focusing on me.

"But you just said—"

"The reason I ended up in that psych ward was because of childhood trauma, lack of healthy coping mechanisms, and substance abuse."

"Then why are the same things happening to me?" I demanded. "My mother didn't throw me in a hole. My brother and sister are still alive. I don't..."

I'd been about to say "I don't have a substance abuse problem", which was technically true at the moment, but it hadn't always been.

"The reason you're seeing those things," said Sylvia with forced calm, obviously stung by my words, "has nothing to do with the house."

"But Simon the bird was a demon, and—"

"None of that shit is real!" Sylvia erupted, slamming a fist on the countertop. "The only demon was my mother, and the only evil came from her untreated mental illness."

"Lester said—"

"Lester Everett? He's beyond senile these days, and even back then he wasn't all there."

I took a deep, shaky breath.

"I saw a body in the well, and I saw you and your siblings burying Simon in the woods," I said, balling my hands into fists to stop them shaking. "I'm forgetting my friends and my sister, and I need you to tell me how to fix this or I'll go insane."

"You don't need teas and crystals, Michelle. You need serious psychological help."

Her anger had faded, replaced by pity, and I couldn't fucking stand it.

"Thanks for nothing," I muttered, and I turned on my heel and left.

Chapter 23

Arriving home to a cold, dark, empty house lowered my spirits even further. Sylvia was not the savior I'd been desperate for. And she was wrong; this house was haunted by more than just the memory of mental breakdowns, and I couldn't be inside it at the moment. Donning a scarf and a knit hat, leaving my phone behind, I set off on another walk, giving the stone well an even wider berth than normal.

Calm down, crazy. There was no skeleton down there. It was all a dream.

Yet my dreams had been feeling more and more real lately. In fact, my dreams were more real than my memories.

Lester's house was as dark as mine. It seemed ominous, so I decided to check on him. I couldn't recall the last time I'd heard from him, but I knew it had been too long; besides, I needed to talk to him about Sylvia. Why hadn't he said anything about her moving back into that house? Did he even know she was still alive?

Nearly tripping over a few empty beer bottles, I made my way to the front door and knocked loudly.

"It's Michelle," I announced. "Hello?"

Backing up a few paces, I peered at the upper floor, hoping to detect movement. Nothing. I knocked again.

"Lester, are you all right?"

Silence. I waited a good few minutes, in case he was moving slowly, but he never came. As a last resort, I tried the knob, but it was locked. Strange how I'd forgotten so much yet clearly remembered him telling me that he never locked his doors. Turning to go, I caught a whiff of decay, and it was accompanied by a sense of foreboding. Dusting off my hands, which suddenly felt filthy, I returned to the forest path.

Despite my low mood, or perhaps because of it, I couldn't seem to stop walking, even to the point of exhaustion. If I was exhausted, then I wouldn't replay the events of today or of Chloe's visit. Keeping a solid pace, I walked all the way to the nearest river crossing, which I knew to be three miles from my house. Over the bridge and along the opposite shore, I continued until I reached the stranger's house I'd only ever glimpsed from afar. Across the water, I could see my own little house, and it brought a smile to my lips.

It was pitch black now. Time to head home.

I had crossed the bridge and was nearing Lester's house again when I heard a soft bird call to my right.

Simon, I thought, and for once the name didn't make me cringe.

All along, I had thought that he was the cause of the trouble in my house, of the way I was losing my connection with my friends and family. I thought he'd wanted to ruin my life. Now, I saw that he'd only been preparing me, helping me to survive on my own, to adapt like he'd never been able to.

The bird call came again, fainter, but his dark shape wasn't in the nearby trees. Through the still-bare branches, slivers of pale water glimmered, and out in the middle of the river, a bird bobbed with the current.

"Simon?"

As I moved closer, I became less certain of what I saw out there. It could've been a bird or a lost sweater or a floating body. Then something flew out of a nearby tree, showering me in what I thought were pine needles but soon realized were feathers. They swirled around me, blinding me, and the next thing I knew, I was on my back, hands clawing wildly at my face until the feathers fell from my eyes.

When I sat up, dark brown and black feathers stuck to my face, neck, collarbone, and bare arms. They itched terribly, but no matter how hard I scratched, the feathers wouldn't budge. In my frenzy to get rid of them, my feet propelled me to the edge of the drop-off. Before I knew it, I had plunged into icy water.

Breath gone, limbs frozen, I remained suspended, unsure which way was up. Precious air escaped from my lips, and I followed the bubbles to the surface, breaking through with an enormous, shuddering gasp.

My hair was caught on something. Frantically, I pulled against it, but my hair tangled tighter with each yank, and my fingers were too cold and stiff to pry myself free. At long last, I managed to twist around so I could see what I was dealing with. My mouth stretched wide in a scream, but all the air inside me was frozen.

Lester was floating facedown, his blue hands curled into claws, one of which gripped my hair. The other was locked around a long, white bone attached to a skeletal hand. Other bits of bone rushed past us – a femur, a vertebra, a skull – carried by the current. Orange fabric clung to them.

Kent.

"Wake – up," I grunted through chattering teeth. "Wake – up!"

Writhing and twisting, I struggled to free my hair, all the time willing myself to wake from this nightmare. But I didn't wake up. This was real.

With an almighty shriek, I finally managed to wrench my hair loose. Immediately, I swam for the shore, from which I had drifted farther and farther away as I fought Lester's grip. Frigid limbs and empty lungs made it nearly impossible, though the shot of adrenaline from seeing the bones helped. By the time I heaved myself up onto the rocks, gasping, every inch of my body had been beaten into heavy numbness.

Only a split-second of internal debate – *Should I try to get him out? Should I call the police?* – and then I was stumbling home. He was already dead. What could I do for him? What I needed was a warm shower, a cup of coffee, and clean, dry clothes.

Someone else must have spotted the floating body, too, because as I ran, flashing blue and white lights cut through the trees in the direction of Lester's house. Their brightness cast spots across my vision, and the sirens jarred my already heightened senses. Thoughts jolted through me with each screeching swoop.

So, there really was a skeleton in the well.
And it really was Kent.
How did Lester find the skeleton?
Who took it out of the well?
Why were my hands dirty?
Did I...

That last thought died before it fully formed as I tripped across the threshold into my house. In the bathroom, I turned the shower to what I thought was lukewarm, peeled off my drenched clothes, and jumped in. The water was so hot it took my breath away. It scalded me until my pores screamed. But I could still feel the iciness of the river and the sticky, itchy feathers. I scratched at my face, my neck, my arms and legs. I scratched until my entire body was bright red, and it wasn't enough. It hurt, but I couldn't stop. I didn't *want* to stop. This skin was unbearable.

When I emerged from the shower half an hour later, the air stung like a thousand pinpricks. Gently, I dried off, leaving the towel as red as my bloody skin. Just the idea of putting on clothes was excruciating, so instead I lay naked in the middle of the living room floor, arms spread like a bird in flight, letting the coolness of the wood soothe my wounds.

I woke up in the exact same position I'd fallen asleep in – legs together, arms stretched wide. Despite my nakedness, I wasn't cold, even though there was frost on the windows and a fresh foot of snow on the deck.

Without looking at myself, I gingerly probed my skin, expecting it to explode with pain. It felt fine, though; maybe even better and smoother than usual. Had the shower and the scratching been a nightmare after all? Slowly, I sat up, then stood, stretching. My body was warm and relaxed, like I'd spent the night at the spa rather than on a hard wood floor.

When I got to the bathroom, I saw that my skin was not only healed, but smooth as porcelain, radiant, blemish-free from top to bottom. The bald patches in my hair, which had been slowly filling in, were now entirely gone, replaced with new, soft, shiny growth, silky and lush as a cashmere sweater. I ran my fingers through it several times in disbelief.

Letting out a little laugh, I spun a full circle, admiring myself. I *felt* better too – lighter, as if I'd been carrying a weight that had dropped away. All the worries that had been bogging me down were gone, leaving only the vague memory that *something* had been bothering me and that it didn't matter anymore.

From head to toe, I was fresh and vibrant.

I was a completely new person.

CHAPTER 24

THE HARSH RINGING OF my phone rudely jerked me out of a blissful doze. Reluctantly, I glanced at the screen. It was a number I didn't recognize, but I answered anyway.

"This is Michelle."

"Oh, thank god!"

"Sorry?"

"I can't believe you actually answered."

"Who is this?"

"It's me."

"Me who?"

"Chloe."

My brain turned the name over and over. It was vaguely familiar, yet I couldn't place it.

"Sorry," I said again. "I think you have the wrong number."

"No, wait, don't hang—"

Jabbing the "End Call" button, I set the phone on my bedside table, sighed, and closed my eyes again. I'd been having a really nice dream. Of course, I couldn't remember it now. Something to do with stars. A swan flying through space? Something like that, anyway.

Right as I was drifting off, the phone rang again. Same number.

"Look, Chloe, I don't know who you're trying to reach—"

"I'm trying to reach *you*! YOU!"

"But I don't know you."

On the other end, Chloe's breathing was ragged. The line became muffled, like she was covering the receiver with her hand, yet I could still hear crying. There was a second voice in the background, a man, comforting her. My heart softened a little.

"Listen," I said gently. "I'm not the person you're looking for. But I hope you're able to find them soon."

Once more, I hung up, vowing to block the number if she called again. My sympathy wasn't deep enough to withstand three wrong numbers, though apparently it *was* deep enough to bring tears to my eyes. Confused, I wiped them away.

It had been a little past noon when I laid down to rest, and now the sun was beginning to sink. Much as I loved the cold weather, I was ready to have longer daylight hours. Not that the darkness ever stopped me from going on walks, which was exactly what I was going to do.

Rolling out of bed, I groaned and stretched and performed a few yoga poses to release the tension in my back and shoulders. Then I crossed the loft to my small upstairs bathroom. I was immensely proud of how it had turned out – cozy and clean in shades of green and gold, like an enchanted forest. I turned my head up and down, left and right, admiring myself in the large mirror. My cheeks were pleasantly pink, and my hair shone with gold undertones. When I braided it, it was almost too thick to tie off.

It was early February, so the temperature was still below freezing most of the time. I donned leggings, a flannel button-down, and boots, but I left the coat, hat, and scarf behind. These days, I found the cold invigorating rather than harsh.

As I was about to head down the spiral staircase, my phone chimed. Starting to get annoyed with this Chloe person, I pulled out my phone to block her, but it wasn't a text. It was an email.

"From: acallawaylmsw@outlook.com
Misha,
Please contact me – this is urgent. Your sister isn't doing well. We're taking her to the hospital, and it would mean a lot if you came to support her. She misses you so much. We all do.
Even though you made it very clear that we're not welcome in your home, and that you don't want our help, we need to at least hear from you every once in a while. One year is too long. We're worried about you, and we love you no matter what.
Love, Daddy"

The fact that it was actually addressed to me using my nickname gave me pause, as did the "callaway" in the stranger's email address. That was *my* last name. Was this person actually related to me? From the way they wrote, they sure seemed to be. I was on the verge of responding when I recalled all those spam emails from supposed relatives who asked for money as soon as you contacted them. Emails along the lines of "I am your long-lost cousin, and I recently came into an inheritance which I'd like to share with you if only you'll give me your Social Security number".

I'd been getting a lot of that spam mail lately, from people named Daniel and Lauren and Christy.

This didn't seem like one of those emails, but better safe than sorry.

"Pass," I said, deleting the email and blocking the sender. "Nice try."

<hr>

I WAS WALKING ALONG the tree-lined forest path, enjoying the fresh air against my face. My pace was brisk, so brisk that I was heating up. I removed my flannel and tied it around my waist, leaving nothing but a thin ribbed camisole. When I reached the bridge, I turned back. Over the dark treetops, the point of my roof peeked out, sturdy and inviting, the sun setting behind it.

Time to go home.

I would never get tired of that thought or that word – *home*.

Acorns snapped under my boots, and pine needles whispered like rustling feathers. The closer I got to home, the faster I went, until finally I emerged from the dense trees and there it was, my beautiful, finished, perfect house. In the gathering darkness, the windows glowed warmly.

Instead of going in the back, I circled around to the front door, thinking about how not that long ago, the door had been nearly destroyed. Doors were amazing, weren't they? Just the idea of being able to shut things out or let them in at your discretion. Suddenly overwhelmed with gratitude for my own house, I strolled through it, opening and shutting every single door, marveling that they were all mine.

Finally coming to rest on the couch, I looked up at the ceiling, then out through the glass wall at the fiery sky and the stark black silhouettes of trees. Then I turned toward the shiny golden perch in the corner, on which a long-tailed bird sat contentedly, its black gaze trained on me.

Smiling, I leaned back and closed my eyes.

At times, it felt like I was forgetting something. Like I'd once had this whole other life with people and places and memories that were now blurs. But I kept telling myself it was all a dream.

I had always been here, and I would always stay here, with Simon.

Kathryn Tennison

Kathryn Tennison is a horror and speculative writer whose work has been published by Bag of Bones Press, Timber Ghost Press, and more, as well as in several anthologies. She currently lives in Arkansas with her husband, two cats, and one enormous fluffy dog. When she's not writing, she enjoys gaming, baking vegan goodies, and curling up with a hot drink and a horror movie. She received her MFA in creative writing from Butler University in Indianapolis.

Instagram & Bluesky: @acaffeinatedkat.

Photo credited to Lori Sparkman.

Acknowledgements

I've been waiting for this since I was 10 years old, and it's hard to believe the moment is here. There are so many people who have helped and believed in me along the way, and I'm proud to be able to finally thank them properly.

Susie and Amanda – thank you for your help navigating this new-to-me world of publishing. I hope my frantic emails didn't bug you too much.

Kassie, Wendy, Caleb, and Emily – thank you for reading the early version of this book and offering advice on home renovations, of which I know very little. It has been a privilege to scare you with my writing for the past six years.

Candace Nola – thank you for taking a chance on me. Thanks also to Christina Pfeiffer and the entire Uncomfortably Dark Horror team for making this book the best it could be and for getting it ready to send out into the world.

My family – thank you for always supporting my dream. At times, I think you believed in my future success more than I believed in it myself. You were and still are my nest, and without you I never would've made it this far.

I'd be remiss if I didn't thank F.A.L.A.L.A. – the Future Author Literary Achievement Lunatic Association – aka my first ever writing group. Shannon and Amanda, all that time we spent in Mrs. Story's classroom at lunchtime acting out scenes in order to find the exact right descriptive words – those hours paid off, and I wouldn't change them for the world.

Finally, thanks and apologies to my husband, who is probably on all kinds of FBI lists due to my questionable internet searches, such as "do human bones float." (They do not.)

Also By Uncomfortably Dark Horror

ANTHOLOGIES
Uncomfortably Dark presents The Baker's Dozen-2021 Dark Dozen anthology & the 2022 Splatterpunk award-winning extreme horror anthology.
Uncomfortably Dark presents Trapped-2022 Dark Dozen anthology that explores themes of horror focused on being trapped in an unspeakable situation.
Uncomfortably Dark presents Dark Disasters-2023 Dark Dozen anthology that explores horrific situations unfolding during natural disasters.
Uncomfortably Dark presents Full Throttle-2025 Dark Dozen Anthology that is a full-blown extreme horror anthology dedicated to survivors of sexual violence.
This anthology contains no scenes of sexual violence.
The Generator-quad collaboration anthology featuring Candace Nola, Eric Butler, M Ennenbach, and Nikolas P. Robinson.
Dark Disturbances- 2024 Uncomfortably Dark Author Sampler Anthology.
Dark Asylum – 2025 Uncomfortably Dark Author Sampler Anthology.

At Midnight, They Feast – 2025 Mini-Halloween Anthology
featuring Cassandra Celia, Candace Nola, and Cat Delani

NOVELS & COLLECTIONS
EPISODES OF VIOLENCE by David Bernstein
DREAMWHISPERS by M Ennenbach
CREMATED REMAINS by M Ennenbach
CUCKOO by M Ennenbach
OLD TOO SOON by Brian Bowyer
BLACKOUT: MICROPOETRY by Brian Bowyer
INNOCENCE ENDS by Nikolas P. Robinson
HAVE A BLAST by Nikolas P. Robinson
COME OUT & PLAY by Patrick Tumblety
ROADS TO RUIN by Brian Bowyer
SUBJECT A by M Ennenbach
OIOS LYKOS by M Ennenbach
STORYSLAVE by Brian Bowyer
VERUM MALUM by Michael R. Collins
PENNYROYAL TEA by Aaron Lebold
THE SHERIFF OF SALEM by Aaron Lebold
GENOCIDE by Aaron Lebold
QUARANTINE by Aaron Lebold
BLASPHEMY by Aaron Lebold
SLENDER BONES IN SACRED SOIL by Fredrick Niles
THIS IS HOW A VILLAIN IS MADE by Amanda Headlee
COFFEE SHOP by Aaron Lebold
ONE FRIGHT ONLY by Patrick Tumblety
WHITE FLIGHT by Peter O'Keefe
BADLANDS by Jason Nickey

Order signed copies and limited-edition hardcovers from
the shop:
https://www.uncomfortablydark.com/shop

Join our Patreon for free books, merch, and more!
https://www.patreon.com/user/membership?u=12231330&view
_as=patron